John Parker Anderson, Frank Thomas Marzials

Life of Charles Dickens

John Parker Anderson, Frank Thomas Marzials

Life of Charles Dickens

ISBN/EAN: 9783337057596

Printed in Europe, USA, Canada, Australia, Japan

Cover: Foto ©Raphael Reischuk / pixelio.de

More available books at **www.hansebooks.com**

LIFE

OF

CHARLES DICKENS

BY

FRANK T. MARZIALS

LONDON
WALTER SCOTT
24 WARWICK LANE, PATERNOSTER ROW

1887

NOTE.

THAT I should have to acknowledge a fairly heavy debt to Forster's " Life of Charles Dickens," and " The Letters of Charles Dickens," edited by his sister-in-law and his eldest daughter, is almost a matter of course ; for these are books from which every present and future biographer of Dickens must perforce borrow in a more or less degree. My work, too, has been much lightened by Mr. Kitton's excellent " Dickensiana."

CONTENTS.

CHAPTER I.

CHAPTER II.

CHAPTER III.

CHAPTER IV.

CHAPTER V.

CHAPTER VI.

CHAPTER VII.

CONTENTS.

CHAPTER XI.

CHAPTER XII.

CHAPTER XIII.

LIFE OF
CHARLES DICKENS.

——◦◦——

EDUCATION is a kind of lottery in which there are good and evil chances, and some men draw blanks and other men draw prizes. And in saying this I do not use the word education in any restricted sense, as applying exclusively to the course of study in school or college; nor certainly, when I speak of prizes, am I thinking of scholarships, exhibitions, fellowships. By education I mean the whole set of circumstances which go to mould a man's character during the apprentice years of his life ; and I call that a prize when those circumstances have been such as to develop the man's powers to the utmost, and to fit him to do best that of which he is best capable. Looked at in this way, Charles Dickens' education, however untoward and unpromising it may often have seemed while in the process, must really be pronounced a prize of value quite inestimable.

His father, John Dickens, held a clerkship in the Navy Pay Office, and was employed in the Portsmouth Dockyard when little Charles first came into the world, at

Landport, in Portsea, on February 7, 1812. Wealth can never have been one of the familiar friends of the household, nor plenty have always sat at its board. Charles had one elder sister, and six other brothers and sisters were afterwards added to the family ; and with eight children, and successive removals from Portsmouth to London, and London to Chatham, and no more than the pay of a Government clerk [1]—pay which not long afterwards dwindled to a pension,—even a better domestic financier than the elder Dickens might have found some difficulty in facing his liabilities. It was unquestionably into a tottering house that the child was born, and among its ruins that he was nurtured.

But through all these early years I can do nothing better than take him for my guide, and walk as it were in his companionship. Perhaps no novelist ever had a keener feeling of the pathos of childhood than Dickens, or understood more fully how real and overwhelming are its sorrows. No one, too, has entered more sympathetically into its ways. And of the child and boy that he himself had once been, he was wont to think very tenderly and very often. Again and again in his writings he reverts to the scenes and incidents and emotions of his earlier days. Sometimes he goes back to his young life directly, speaking as of himself. More often he goes back to it indirectly, placing imaginary children and boys in the position he had once occupied. Thus it is almost possible, by judiciously

---

[1] £200 a year "without extras" from 1815 to 1820, and then £350. See "Childhood and Youth of Charles Dickens," by Robert Langton, a very valuable monograph.

selecting from his works, and using such keys as we . possess, to construct as it were a kind of autobiography. Nor, if we make due allowance for the great writer's tendency to idealize the past, and intensify its humorous and pathetic aspects, need we at all fear that the self-written story of his life should convey a false impression.

He was but two years old when his father left Portsea for London, and but four when a second migration took the family to Chatham. Here we catch our first glimpse of him, in his own word-painting, as a " very queer small boy," a small boy who was sickly and delicate, and could take but little part in the rougher sports of his school companions, but read much, as sickly boys will—read the novels of the older novelists in a " blessed little room," a kind of palace of enchantment, where "'Roderick Random,' ' Peregrine Pickle,' ' Humphrey Clinker,' ' Tom Jones,' ' The Vicar of Wakefield,' ' Don Quixote, ' Gil Blas,' and ' Robinson Crusoe,' came out, a glorious host, to keep him company." And the queer small boy had read Shakespeare's " Henry IV.," too, and knew all about Falstaff's robbery of the travellers at Gad's Hill, on the rising ground between Rochester and Gravesend, and all about mad Prince Henry's pranks ; and, what was more, he had determined that when he came to be a man, and had made his way in the world, he should own the house called Gad's Hill Place, with the old associations of its site, and its pleasant outlook over Rochester and over the low-lying levels by the Thames. Was that a child's dream ? The man's tenacity and steadfast strength of purpose turned it into fact. The house became the home of his later life. It was there that he died.

But death was a long way forward in those old Chatham days ; nor, as the time slipped by, and his father's pecuniary embarrassments began to thicken, and make the forward ways of life more dark and difficult, could the purchase of Gad's Hill Place have seemed much less remote. There is one of Dickens' works which was his own special favourite, the most cherished, as he tells us, among the offspring of his brain. That work is "David Copperfield." Nor can there be much difficulty in discovering why it occupied such an exceptional position in "his heart of hearts ;" for in its pages he had enshrined the deepest memories of his own childhood and youth. Like David Copperfield, he had known what it was to be a poor, neglected lad, set to rough, uncongenial work, with no more than a mechanic's surroundings and outlook, and having to fend for himself in the miry ways of the great city. Like David Copperfield, he had formed a very early acquaintance with debts and duns, and been initiated into the mysteries and sad expedients of shabby poverty. Like David Copperfield, he had been made free of the interior of a debtor's prison. Poor lad, he was not much more than ten or eleven years old when he left Chatham, with all the charms that were ever after to live so brightly in his recollection,—the gay military pageantry, the swarming dockyard, the shifting sailor life, the delightful walks in the surrounding country, the enchanted room, tenanted by the first fairy day-dreams of his genius, the day-school, where the master had already formed a good opinion of his parts, giving him Goldsmith's "Bee" as a keepsake. This pleasant land he left for a dingy house in a dingy London suburb,

with squalor for companionship, no teaching but
the teaching of the streets, and all around and above
him the depressing hideous atmosphere of debt.
With what inimitable humour and pathos has he told
the story of these darkest days! Substitute John
Dickens for Mr. Micawber, and Mrs. Dickens for Mrs.
Micawber, and make David Copperfield a son of Mr.
Micawber, a kind of elder Wilkins, and let little Charles
Dickens be that son—and then you will have a record,
true in every essential respect, of the child's life at this
period. "Poor Mrs. Micawber! she said she had tried
to exert herself; and so, I have no doubt, she had. The
centre of the street door was perfectly covered with a
great brass-plate, on which was engraved 'Mrs. Micawber's Boarding Establishment for Young Ladies;' but I
never found that any young lady had ever been to school
there; or that any young lady ever came, or proposed to
come; or that the least preparation was ever made to
receive any young lady. The only visitors I ever saw or
heard of were creditors. *They* used to come at all hours,
and some of them were quite ferocious." Even such a plate,
bearing the inscription, *Mrs. Dickens's Establishment*,
ornamented the door of a house in Gower Street North,
where the family had hoped, by some desperate effort, to
retrieve its ruined fortunes. Even so did the pupils refuse
the educational advantages offered to them, though little
Charles went from door to door in the neighbourhood,
carrying hither and thither the most alluring circulars.
Even thus was the place besieged by assiduous and
angry duns. And when, in the ordinary course of such
sad stories, Mr. Dickens is arrested for debt, and carried

off to the Marshalsea prison,[1] he moralizes over the event
in precisely the same strain as Mr. Micawber, using, indeed,
the very same words, and calls on his son, with many
tears, "to take warning by the Marshalsea, and to observe
that if a man had twenty pounds a year, and spent nineteen pounds nineteen shillings and sixpence, he would be
happy; but that a shilling spent the other way would
make him wretched."

The son was taking note of other things besides these
moral apothegms, and reproduced, in after days, with a
quite marvellous detail and fidelity, all the incidents of
his father's incarceration.   Probably, too, he was beginning, as children will, almost unconsciously, to form some
estimate of his father's character.   And a very queer
study in human nature *that* must have been, giving
Dickens, when once he had mastered it, a most exceptional insight into the ways of impecuniosity.   Charles
Lamb, as we all remember, divided mankind into two
races, the mighty race of the borrowers, and the mean
race of the lenders ; and expatiated, with a whimsical
and charming eloquence, upon the greatness of one
Bigod, who had been as a king among those who by
process of loan obtain possession of other people's
money.   Shift the line of division a little, so that instead
of separating borrowers and lenders, it separates those
who pay their debts from those who do not pay them,
and then Dickens the elder may succeed to something of
Bigod's kingship.   He was of the great race of debtors,

---

[1] Mr. Langton appears to doubt whether John Dickens was not
imprisoned in the King's Bench.   But this seems scarcely a point on
which Dickens himself can have been mistaken.

possessing especially that *ideal* quality of mind on which Lamb laid such stress. Imagination played the very mischief with him. He had evidently little grasp of fact, and moved in a kind of haze, through which all clear outlines would show blurred and unreal. Sometimes— most often, perhaps—that haze would be irradiated with sanguine visionary hopes and expectations. Sometimes it would be fitfully darkened with all the horrors of despair. But whether in gloom or gleam, the realities of his position would be lost. He never, certainly, con- tracted a debt which he did not mean honourably to pay. But either he had never possessed the faculty of forming a just estimate of future possibilities, or else, through the indulgence of what may be called a vague habit of thought, he had lost the power of seeing things as they are. Thus all his excellencies and good gifts were neutralized at this time, so far as his family were con- cerned, and went for practically nothing. He was, according to his son's testimony, full of industry, most conscientious in the discharge of any business, unweary- ing in loving patience and solicitude when those bound to him by blood or friendship were ill or in trouble, "as kind-hearted and generous a man as ever lived in the world." Yet as debts accumulated, and accommodation bills shed their baleful shadow on his life, and duns grew many and furious, he became altogether immersed in mean money troubles, and suffered the son who was to shed such lustre on his name to remain for a time with- out the means of learning, and to sink first into a little household drudge, and then into a mere warehouse boy.) So little Charles, aged from eleven to twelve, first blacked boots, and minded the younger children, and ran messages, and effected the family purchases—which can have been no pleasant task in the then state of the family credit,—and made very close acquaintance with the inside of the pawnbrokers' shops, and with the purchasers of second-hand books, disposing, among other things, of the little store of books he loved so well ; and then, when his father was imprisoned, ran more messages hither and thither, and shed many childish tears in his father's company—the father doubtless regarding the tears as a tribute to his eloquence, though, heaven knows, there were other things to cry over besides his sonorous periods. After which a connection, James Lamert by name, who had lived with the family before they moved from Camden Town to Gower Street, and was manager of a worm-eaten, rat-riddled blacking business, near old Hungerford Market, offered to employ the lad, on a salary of some six shillings a week, or thereabouts. The duties which commanded these high emoluments consisted of the tying up and labelling of blacking pots. At first Charles, in consideration probably of his relationship to the manager, was allowed to do his tying, clipping, and pasting in the counting-house. But soon this arrangement fell through, as it naturally would, and he descended to the companionship of the other lads, similarly employed, in the warehouse below. They were not bad boys, and one of them, who bore the name of Bob Fagin, was very kind to the poor little better-nurtured outcast, once, in a sudden attack of illness, applying hot blacking-bottles to his side with much tenderness. But, of course, they were rough and quite uncultured, and the sensitive, bookish, imaginative child felt that there was something uncongenial and degrading in being compelled to associate with them. Nor, though he had already sufficient strength of character to learn to do his work well, did he ever regard the work itself as anything but unsuitable, and almost discreditable. Indeed it may be doubted whether the iron of that time did not unduly rankle and fester as it entered into his soul, and whether the scar caused by the wound was altogether quite honourable. He seems to have felt, in connection with his early employment in a warehouse, a sense of shame such as would be more fittingly associated with the commission of an unworthy act. That he should not have habitually referred to the subject in after life, may readily be understood. But why he should have kept unbroken silence about it for long years, even with his wife, even with so very close a friend as Forster, is less clear. And in the terms used, when the revelation was finally made to Forster, there has always, I confess, appeared to me to be a tone of exaggeration. " My whole nature," he says, "was so penetrated with grief and humiliation, . . . that even now, famous and caressed and happy, I often forget in my dreams that I have a dear wife and children ; even that I am a man, and wander desolately back to that time of my life." And again : " From that hour until this, at which I write, no word of that part of my childhood, which I have now gladly brought to a close, has passed my lips to any human being. . . . I have never, until I now impart it to this paper, in any burst of confidence with any one, my own wife not excepted, raised the turtain I then dropped, thank God." Great part, perhaps the greatest part, of

Dickens' success as a writer, came from the sympathy and power with which he showed how the lower walks of life no less than the higher are often fringed with beauty. I have never been able to entirely divest myself of a slight feeling of the incongruous in reading what he wrote about the warehouse episode in his career.

At first, when he began his daily toil at the blacking business, some poor dregs of family life were left to the child. His father was at the Marshalsea. But his mother and brothers and sisters were, to use his own words, "still encamped, with a young servant girl from Chatham workhouse, in the two parlours in the emptied house in Gower Street North." And there he lived with them, in much "hugger-mugger," merely taking his humble midday meal in nomadic fashion, on his own account. Soon, however, his position became even more forlorn. The paternal creditors proved insatiable. The gipsy home in Gower Street had to be broken up. Mrs. Dickens and the children went to live at the Marshalsea. Little Charles was placed under the roof—it cannot be called under the care—of a "reduced old lady," dwelling in Camden Town, who must have been a clever and prophetic old lady if she anticipated that her diminutive lodger would one day give her a kind of indirect unenviable immortality by making her figure, under the name of "Mrs. Pipchin," in "Dombey and Son." Here the boy seems to have been left almost entirely to his own devices. He spent his Sundays in the prison, and, to the best of his recollection, his lodgings at "Mrs. Pipchin's" were paid for. Otherwise, he "found himself," in childish fashion, out of the six or seven weekly shillings, breakfasting on two pennyworth of bread and milk, and supping on a penny loaf and a bit of cheese, and dining hither and thither, as his boy's appetite dictated—now, sensibly enough, on à la mode beef or a saveloy; then, less sensibly, on pudding; and anon not dining at all, the wherewithal having been expended on some morning treat of cheap stale pastry. But are not all these things, the lad's shifts and expedients, his sorrows and despair, his visits to the public-house, where the kindly publican's wife stoops down to kiss the pathetic little face—are they not all written in " David Copperfield "? And if so be that I have a reader unacquainted with that peerless book, can I do better than recommend him, or her, to study therein the story of Dickens' life at this particular time?

At last the child's solitude and sorrows seem to have grown unbearable. His fortitude broke down. One Sunday night he appealed to his father, with many tears, on the subject, not of his employment, which he seems to have accepted at the time manfully, but of his forlornness and isolation. The father's kind, thoughtless heart was touched. A back attic was found for Charles near the Marshalsea, at Lant Street, in the Borough—where Bob Sawyer, it will be remembered, afterwards invited Mr. Pickwick to that disastrous party. The boy moved into his new quarters with the same feeling of elation as if he had been entering a palace.

The change naturally brought him more fully into the prison circle. He used to breakfast there every morning, before going to the warehouse, and would spend the larger portion of his spare time among the inmates. Nor do Mr. Dickens and his family, and Charles, who is to us the

family's most important member, appear to have been rela-
tively at all uncomfortable while under the shadow of the
Marshalsea.   There is in "David Copperfield" a passage
of inimitable humour, where Mr. Micawber, enlarging on
the pleasures of imprisonment for debt, apostrophizes the
King's Bench Prison as being the place " where, for the first
time in many revolving years, the overwhelming pressure of
pecuniary liabilities was not proclaimed from day to day,
by importunate voices declining to vacate the passage;
where there was no knocker on the door for any creditor
to appeal to ; where personal service of process was not
required, and detainers were lodged merely at the gate."
There is a similar passage in " Little Dorrit," where the
tipsy medical practitioner of the Marshalsea comforts Mr.
Dorrit in his affliction by saying : "We are quiet here;
we don't get badgered here ; there's no knocker here, sir,
to be hammered at by creditors, and bring a man's heart
into his mouth.   Nobody comes here to ask if a man's
at home, and to say he'll stand on the door-mat till
he is.   Nobody writes threatening letters about money
to this place.   It's freedom, sir, it's freedom !"   One
smiles as one reads; and it adds a pathos, I think, to
the smile, to find that these are records of actual experience.   The Marshalsea prison was to Mr. Dickens a
haven of peace, and to his household a place of plenty.
Not only could he pursue his career there untroubled by
fears of arrest, but he exercised among the other "gentlemen gaol-birds" a supremacy, a kind of kingship, such as
that to which Charles Lamb referred.   They recognized
in him the superior spirit, ready of pen, and affluent of
speech, and with a certain grandeur in his conviviality.

He it was who drew up their memorial to George of
England on an occasion no less important than the royal
birthday, when they, the monarch's "unfortunate subjects"—so they were described in the memorial—
besought the king's "gracious majesty," of his "well-
known munificence," to grant them a something towards
the drinking of the royal health. (Ah, with what keen
eyes and penetrative genius did little Charles, from his
corner, watch the strange sad stream of humanity that
trickled through the room, and may be said to have
smeared its approval of that petition !) And while Mr.
Dickens was enjoying his prison honours, he was also
enjoying his Admiralty pension,[1] which was not forfeited
by his imprisonment ; and his wife and children were
consequently enjoying a larger measure of the necessaries
of life than had been theirs for many a month. So all
went on merrily enough at the Marshalsea.

But even under the old law, imprisonment for debt
did not always last for ever. A legacy, and the Insolvent
Debtors Act, enabled Mr. Dickens to march out of
durance, in some sort with the honours of war, after a few
months' incarceration—this would be early in 1824 ;—and
he went with his family, including Charles, to lodge with the
" Mrs. Pipchin " already mentioned. Charles meanwhile
still toiled on in the blacking warehouse, now removed to
Chandos Street, Covent Garden ; and had reached such
skill in the tying, pasting, and labelling of the bottles,
that small crowds used to collect at the window for the
purpose of watching his deft fingers. There was pride in

[1] According to Mr. Langton's dates, he would still be drawing

this, no doubt, but also humiliation; and release was at hand. His father and Lamert quarrelled about something — about *what*, Dickens seems never to have known—and he was sent home. Mrs. Dickens acted the part of the peacemaker on the next day, probably feeling that amid the shadowy expectations on which she and her husband had subsisted for so long, even six or seven shillings a week was something tangible, and not to be despised. Yet in spite of this, he did not return to the business. His father decided that he should go to school. "I do not write resentfully or angrily," said Dickens, in the confidential communication made long afterwards to Forster, and to which reference has already been made; "but I never afterwards forgot, I never shall forget, I never can forget, that my mother was warm for my being sent back."

The mothers of great men is a subject that has been handled often, and eloquently. How many of those who have achieved distinction can trace their inherited gifts to a mother's character, and their acquired gifts to a mother's teaching and influence. Mrs. Dickens seems not to have been a mother of this stamp. She scarcely, I fear, possessed those admirable qualities of mind and heart which one can clearly recognize as having borne fruit in the greatness and goodness of her famous son. So far as I can discover, she exercised no influence upon him at all. Her name hardly appears in his biographies. He never, that I can recollect, mentions her in his correspondence; only refers to her on the rarest occasions. And perhaps, on the whole, this is not to be wondered at, if we accept the constant tradition that she had, unknown to herself, sat to her son for the portrait of Mrs. Nickleby, and suggested to him the main traits in the character of that inconsequent and not very wise old lady. Mrs. Nickleby, I take it, was not the kind of person calculated to form the mind of a boy of genius. As well might one expect some very domestic bird to teach an eaglet how to fly.

The school to which our callow eaglet was sent (in the spring or early summer of 1824), belonged emphatically to the old school of schools. It bore the goodly name of *Wellington House Academy*, and was situated in Mornington Place, near the Hampstead Road. A certain Mr. Jones held chief rule there; and as more than fifty years have now elapsed since Dickens' connection with the establishment ceased, I trust there may be nothing libellous in giving further currency to his statement, or rather, perhaps, to his recorded impression,[1] that the head master's one qualification for his office was dexterity in the use of the cane;—especially as another "old boy" corroborates that impression, and declares Mr. Jones to have been "a most ignorant fellow, and a mere tyrant." Dickens, however, escaped with comparatively little beating, because he was a day-boy, and sound policy dictated that day-boys, who had facilities for carrying home their complaints, should be treated with some leniency. So he had to get his learning without tears, which was not at all considered the orthodox method in the good old days; and, indeed, I doubt if he finally took away from Wellington House Academy very much of the book knowledge that would tell in a modern com-

[1] See paper entitled " Our School."

petitive examination. For though in his own account of
the school it is implied that he resumed his interrupted
studies with Virgil, and was, before he left, head boy, and
the possessor of many prizes, yet this is not corroborated
by the evidence of his surviving fellow pupils ; nor can
we, of course, in the face of their direct counter evidence,
treat statements made in a fictitious or half-fictitious
narrative as if made in what professed to be a sober
autobiography. Dickens, I repeat, seems to have acquired
a very scant amount of classic lore while under the instruction of Mr. Jones, and not too much lore of any
kind. But if he learned little, he observed much. He
thoroughly mastered the humours of the place, just as he
had mastered the humours of the Marshalsea. He had
got to know all about the masters, and all about the boys,
and all about the white mice—of which there were many
in various stages of civilization. He acquired, in short,
a fund of school knowledge that seemed inexhaustible,
and on which he drew again and again, with the most excellent results, in "David Copperfield," in "Dombey," in
such inimitable short papers as "Old Cheeseman." And
while thus, half unconsciously perhaps, assimilating the
very life of the school, he was himself a thorough schoolboy,
bright, alert, intelligent ; taking part in all fun and frolic ;
amply indemnifying himself for his enforced abstinence
from childish games during the dreary warehouse days;
good at recitations and mimic plays; and already possessed of a reputation among his peers as a writer of
tales.

CHAPTER II.

DICKENS cannot have been very long at Wellington House Academy, for before May, 1827, he had been at another school near Brunswick Square, and had also obtained, and quitted, some employment in the office of a solicitor in New Square, Lincoln's Inn Fields. It seems clear, therefore, that the whole of his school life might easily be computed in months; and in May, 1827, it will be remembered, he was still but a lad of fifteen. At that date he entered the office of a second solicitor, in Gray's Inn this time, on a salary of thirteen shillings and sixpence a week, afterwards increased to fifteen shillings. Here he remained till November, 1828, again picking up a good deal of information that cannot perhaps be regarded as strictly legal, but such as he was afterwards able to turn to admirable account. He would seem to have studied the profession exhaustively in all its branches, from the topmost Tulkinghorns and Perkers, to the lowest pettifoggers like Pell and Brass, and also to have given particular attention to the parasites of the law—the Guppys and Chucksters; and altogether to have stored his mind, as he had done at school, with a series of invaluable notes and observations. All very well, no doubt,

as we look at the matter now.   But then it must often
have seemed to the ambitious, energetic lad, that he was
wasting his time.   Was he to remain for ever a lawyer's
clerk who has not the means to be an articled clerk, and
who can never, therefore, aspire to become a full-blown
solicitor?   Was he to spend the future obscurely in the
dingy purlieus of the law?   His father, in whose career
"something," as Mr. Micawber would have said, had at
last "turned up," was now a reporter for the press.
The son determined to be a reporter too.

He threw himself into this new career with characteristic energy.   Of course a reporter is not made in a day.
It takes many months of drudgery to obtain such skill in
shorthand as shall enable the pen of the ready-writer to
keep up with the winged words of speech, and make dots
and lines that shall be readable.   Dickens laboured hard
to acquire the art.   In the intervals of his work he made
it a kind of holiday task to attend the Reading-room of
the British Museum, and so remedy the defects in the
literary part of his education.   But the best powers of his
mind were directed to "Gurney's system of shorthand."
And in time he had his reward.   He earned and justified
the reputation of being one of the best reporters of his
day.

I shall not quote the autobiographical passages in
"David Copperfield" which bear on the difficulties of
stenography.   The book is in everybody's hands.   But I
cannot forego the pleasure of brightening my pages with
Dickens' own description of his experiences as a reporter,
a description contained in one of those charming felicitous
speeches of his which are almost as unique in kind as his

novels. Speaking in May, 1865, as chairman of a public
dinner on behalf of the Newspaper Press Fund, he said :
" I have pursued the calling of a reporter under circumstances of which many of my brethren at home in
England here, many of my modern successors, can form
no adequate conception. I have often transcribed for
the printer, from my shorthand notes, important public
speeches, in which the strictest accuracy was required,
and a mistake in which would have been, to a young man,
severely compromising, writing on the palm of my hand,
by the light of a dark lantern, in a post-chaise and four,
galloping through a wild country, and through the dead of
the night, at the then surprising rate of fifteen miles an
hour. The very last time I was at Exeter, I strolled into the
castle-yard there to identify, for the amusement of a friend,
the spot on which I once took, as we used to call it, an
election speech of my noble friend Lord Russell, in the
midst of a lively fight maintained by all the vagabonds in
that division of the county, and under such pelting rain,
that I remember two good-natured colleagues, who
chanced to be at leisure, held a pocket-handkerchief over
my note-book, after the manner of a State canopy in an
ecclesiastical procession. I have worn my knees by
writing on them on the old back row of the old gallery in the
old House of Commons ; and I have worn my feet by
standing to write in a preposterous pen in the old House
of Lords, where we used to be huddled together like so
many sheep, kept in waiting, say, until the woolsack might
want re-stuffing. Returning home from excited political
meetings in the country to the waiting press in London, I
do verily believe I have been upset in almost every de-

scription of vehicle known in this country. I have been, in my time, belated in miry by-roads, towards the small hours, forty or fifty miles from London, in a wheel-less carriage, with exhausted horses, and drunken postboys, and have got back in time for publication, to be received with never-forgotten compliments by the late Mr. Black, coming in the broadest of Scotch from the broadest of hearts I ever knew."

What shall I add to this? That the papers on which he was engaged as a reporter, were *The True Sun, The Mirror of Parliament,* and *The Morning Chronicle;* that long afterwards, little more than two years before his death, when addressing the journalists of New York, he gave public expression to his "grateful remembrance of a calling that was once his own," and declared, "to the wholesome training of severe newspaper work, when I was a very young man, I constantly refer my first success;" that his income as a reporter appears latterly to have been some five guineas a week, of course in addition to expenses and general breakages and damages; that there is independent testimony to his exceptional quickness in reporting and transcribing, and to his intelligence in condensing; that to an observer so keen and apt, the experiences of his business journeys in those more picturesque and eventful ante-railway days must have been invaluable; and, finally, that his connection with journalism lasted far into 1836, and so did not cease till some months after " Pickwick" had begun to add to the world's store of merriment and laughter.

But I have not really reached " Pickwick" yet, nor anything like it. That master-work was not also a first work.

With all Dickens' genius, he had to go through some apprenticeship in the writer's art before coming upon the public as the most popular novelist of his time. Let us go back for a little to the twilight before the full sunrise, nay, to the earliest streak upon the greyness of night, to his first original published composition. Dickens himself, and in his preface to "Pickwick" too, has told us somewhat about that first paper of his; how it was "dropped steal- thily one evening at twilight, with fear and trembling, into a dark letter-box, in a dark office, up a dark court in Fleet Street;" how it was accepted, and "appeared in all the glory of print;" and how he was so filled with pleasure and pride on purchasing a copy of the magazine in which it was published, that he went into Westminster Hall to hide the tears of joy that would come into his eyes. The paper thus joyfully wept over was originally entitled "A Dinner at Poplar Walk," and now bears, among the "Sketches by Boz," the name of "Mr. Minns and his Cousin"; the periodical in which it was published was *The Old Monthly Magazine,* and the date of publication was January 1, 1834.

"A Dinner at Poplar Walk" may be pronounced a very fairly told tale. It is, no doubt, always easy to be wise after the event, in criticism particularly easy, and when once a writer has achieved success, there is but too little difficulty in showing that his earlier productions were prophetic of his future greatness. At the risk, however, of incurring a charge of this kind, I repeat that Dickens' first story is well told, and that the editor of *The Old Monthly Magazine* showed due discernment in accepting it and encouraging his unknown contributor to further efforts. Quite apart from the fact that the author was only a young fellow of some two or three and twenty, both this first story and the stories that followed it in *The Old Monthly Magazine*, during 1834 and the early part of 1835, possessed qualities of a very remarkable kind. So also did the humorous descriptive papers shortly afterwards published in *The Evening Chronicle*, papers that, with the stories, now compose the book known as "Sketches by Boz." Sir Arthur Helps, speaking of Dickens, just after Dickens' death,[1] said, "His powers of observation were almost unrivalled. . . . Indeed, I have said to myself when I have been with him, he sees and observes nine facts for any two that I see and observe." This particular faculty is, I think, almost as clearly discernible in the "Sketches" as in the author's later and greater works. London—its sins and sorrows, its gaieties and amusements, its suburban gentilities, and central squalor, the aspects of its streets, and the humours of the dingier classes among its inhabitants,—all this had certainly never been so seen and described before. The power of exact minute delineation lavished upon the picture is admirable. Again, the dialogue in the dramatic parts is natural, well-conducted, characteristic, and so used as to help, not impede, the narrative. The speech, for instance, of Mr. Bung, the broker's man, is a piece of very good Dickens. Of course there is humour, and very excellent fooling some of it is ; and equally, of course, there is pathos, and some of that is not bad. Do I mean at all that this earlier work stands on the same level of excellence as the masterpieces of the writer ? Clearly not. It

[1] *Macmillan's Magazine*, July, 1870.

were absurd to expect the stripling, half-furtively coming forward, first without a name at all, and then under the pseudonym of Boz,[1] to write with the superb practised ease and mastery of the Charles Dickens who penned "David Copperfield." By dint of doing blacksmith's work, says the French proverb, one becomes a blacksmith. The artist, like the handicraftsman, must learn his art. Much in the "Sketches" betrays inexperience ; or, perhaps, it would be more just to say, comparative clumsiness of hand. The descriptions, graphic as they undoubtedly are, lack for the most part the final imaginative touch ; the kind of inbreathing of life which afterwards gave such individual charm to Dickens' word-painting. The humour is more obvious, less delicate, turns too readily on the claim of the elderly spinster to be considered young, and the desire of all spinsters to get married. The pathos is often spoilt by over-emphasis and declamation. It lacks simplicity.

For the "Sketches" published in *The Old Monthly Magazine*, Dickens got nothing, beyond the pleasure of seeing himself in print. The *Chronicle* treated him somewhat more liberally, and, on his application, increased his salary, giving him, in view of his original contributions, seven guineas a week, instead of the five guineas which he had been drawing as a reporter. Not a particularly brilliant augmentation, perhaps, and one at which he must often have smiled in after years, when his pen was dropping gold as well as ink. Still, the addition to his income was substantial, and the son of John Dickens must

[1] It was the pet name of one of his brothers ; that was why he took it.

3

always, I imagine, have been in special need of money. Moreover the circumstances of the next few months would render any increased earnings doubly pleasant. For Dickens was shortly after this engaged to be married to Miss Catherine Hogarth, the daughter of one of his fellow-workers on the *Chronicle*. There had been, so Forster tells us, a previous very shadowy love affair in his career,—an affair so visionary indeed, and boyish, as scarcely to be worthy of mention in this history, save for three facts : first, that his devotion, dreamlike as it was, seems to have had love's highest practical effect in inducing him to throw his whole strength into the study of shorthand ; secondly, that the lady of his love appears to have had some resemblance to Dora, the child-wife of David Copperfield ; and thirdly, that he met her again long years afterwards, when time had worked its changes, and the glamour of love had left his eyes, and that to that meeting we owe the passages in "Little Dorrit" relating to poor Flora. This, however, is a parenthesis. The engagement to Miss Hogarth was neither shadowy nor unreal—an engagement only in dreamland. Better for both, perhaps—who knows ?—if it had been. Ah me, if one could peer into the future, how many weddings there are at which tears would be more appropriate than smiles and laughter ! Would Charles Dickens and Catherine Hogarth have foreborne to plight their troth, one wonders, if they could have foreseen how slowly and surely the coming years were to sunder their hearts and lives ?—They were married on the 2nd of April, 1836.

This date again leads me to a time subsequent to the publication of the first number of "Pickwick," which had

appeared a day or two before ; — and again I refrain
from dealing with that great book. For before I do so,
I wish to pause a brief space to consider what manner of
man Charles Dickens was when he suddenly broke on
the world in his full popularity; and also what were the
influences, for good and evil, which his early career had
exercised upon his character and intellect.

What manner of man he was ? In outward aspect all
accounts agree that he was singularly, noticeably pre-
possessing—bright, animated, eager, with energy and
talent written in every line of his face. Such he was
when Forster saw him, on the occasion of their first
meeting, when Dickens was acting as spokesman for the
insurgent reporters engaged on the *Mirror.* So Carlyle, .
who met him at dinner shortly after this, and was no
flatterer, sketches him for us with a pen of unwonted
kindliness. "He is a fine little fellow—Boz, I think.
Clear, blue, intelligent eyes, eyebrows that he arches
amazingly, large protrusive rather loose mouth, a face of
most extreme *mobility*, which he shuttles about—eyebrows,
eyes, mouth and all—in a very singular manner while
speaking. Surmount this with a loose coil of common-
coloured hair, and set it on a small compact figure, very
small, and dressed *à la* D'Orsay rather than well—this is
Pickwick. For the rest, a quiet, shrewd-looking little
fellow, who seems to guess pretty well what he is and
what others are." [1] Is not this a graphic little picture,
and characteristic even to the touch about D'Orsay, the
dandy French Count ? For Dickens, like the young men

[1] Froude's "Thomas Carlyle : A History of his Life in
London."

of the time—Disraeli, Bulwer, and the rest—was a great
fop. We, of these degenerate days, shall never see again
that antique magnificence in coloured velvet waistcoats.

But to return. Dickens, it need scarcely be said, had
by this long out-lived the sickliness of his earlier years.
The hardships and trials of his childhood and boyhood
had served but to brace his young manhood, knitting the
frame and strengthening the nerves. Light and small, as
Carlyle describes him, he was wiry and very active, and
could bear without injury an amount of intellectual work
and bodily fatigue that would have killed many men of
seemingly stronger build. And as what might have
seemed unfortunate in his youth had helped perchance
to develop his physical powers, so had it assisted to
strengthen his character and foster his genius. I go back
here to the point from which I started. No doubt a
weaker man would have been crushed by such a youth.
He would have been indolently content to remain a
warehouse drudge, would have listlessly fallen into his
father's ways about money, would have had no ambition
beyond his desk and salary as a lawyer's clerk, would
have never cared to piece together and supplement the
scattered scraps of his education, would have rested on
his oars when he had once shot into the waters of ordinary journalism. With Dickens it was not so. The
alchemy of a fine nature had transmuted his disadvantages
into gold. To him the lessons of such a childhood and
boyhood as he had had, were energy, self-reliance, a
determination to overcome all obstacles, to fight the
battles of life, in all honour and rectitude, so as to win.
From the muddle of his father's affairs he had taken away

a lesson of method, order, and punctuality in business and other arrangements. " What is worth doing at all is worth doing well," was not only one of his favourite maxims—it was the rule of his life.

And for what was to be his life work, what better pre-paration could there have been than that which he received? I am far from recommending warehouses, squalid solitary lodgings, pawnshops, debtors' prisons,—if such could now be found,—ill-conducted private schools, —which probably could be found,—attorneys' offices, and the hand-to-mouth of journalism, as constituting generally the highest ideal of a liberal education. I am equally far from asserting that the majority of men do not require more training of a purely scholastic kind than fell to Dickens' lot. But Dickens was not a bookish man. His genius did not lie in that direction. To have forced him unduly into the world of books would have made him, doubtless, an average scholar, but might have weak-ened his hold on life. Such a risk was certainly not worth the running. Fate arranged it otherwise. What he was above all was a student of the world of men, a passionately keen observer of the ways of humanity. Men were to be his books, his special branch of knowledge ; and in order to graduate and take high honours in that school, I repeat, he could have had no better training. Not only had he passed through a range of most unwonted expe-riences, experiences calculated to quicken to the uttermost his superb faculties of observation and insight ; but he had been placed in sympathetic communication with a strange assortment of characters, lying quite out of the usual ken of the literary classes. Knowledge and sympathy, the seeing eye and the feeling heart—were these nothing to have acquired?

That so abnormal an education can have been entirely without drawbacks, it is no part of my purpose to affirm. Tossed, as one may say, to sink or swim amid the waves of life, where those waves ran turbid and brackish, Dickens had emerged strengthened, triumphant. But that some little signs should not remain of the straining and effort with which he had won the land, was scarcely to be expected. He himself, in his more confidential communications with Forster, seems to avow a consciousness that, this was so; and Forster, though he speaks guardedly, lovingly, appears to be of opinion that a certain self-asser-tiveness and fierce intolerance of advice or control [1] occasionally discernible in his friend, might justly be attributed to the harsh influence of early struggles and privations. But what then? That system of education has yet to be devised which shall mould this poor human clay of ours into flawless shapes of use and beauty. A man may be considered fortunate indeed, when his training has left in him only what the French call the " defects

---

[1] " I have heard Dickens described by those who knew him," says Mr. Edmund Yates, in his "Recollections," "as aggressive, impe-rious, and intolerant, and I can comprehend the accusation. . . . He was imperious in the sense that his life was conducted on the *sic volo sic jubeo* principle, and that everything gave way before him. The society in which he mixed, the hours which he kept, the opinions which he held, his likes and dislikes, his ideas of what should or should not be, were all settled by himself, not merely for himself, but for all those brought into connection with him, and it was never imagined they could be called in question. . . . He had immense powers of will."

of his virtues," that is, the exaggeration of his good qualities till they turn into faults. Without his immense
strength of purpose and iron will, Dickens might never
have emerged from obscurity, and the world would have
been very distinctly the poorer. One cannot be very
sorry that he possessed these gifts in excess.

°And now, at last, having slightly sketched the history
of his earlier years, and endeavoured to show, however
imperfectly, what influences had gone to the formation of
his character, I proceed to consider the book that lifted
him to fame and fortune. The years of apprenticeship
are over, and the master-workman brings forth his finished
work in its flower of perfection. Let us study " Pickwick."

CHAPTER III.

DICKENS has told us, in his preface to the later editions, much of how " Pickwick" came to be projected and published. It was in this wise : Seymour, a caricaturist of very considerable merit, though not, as we should now consider, in the first rank of the great caricaturists, had proposed to Messrs. Chapman and Hall, then just starting on their career as publishers, a " series of Cockney sporting plates." Messrs. Chapman and Hall entertained the idea favourably, but opined that the plates would require illustrative letter-press ; and casting about for some suitable author, bethought themselves of Dickens, whose tales and sketches had been exciting some little sensation in the world of journalism ; and who had, indeed, already written for the firm a story, the " Tuggs at Ramsgate," which may be read among the " Sketches." Accordingly Mr. Hall called on Dickens for the purpose of proposing the scheme. This would be in 1835, towards the latter end of the year ; and Dickens, who had apparently left the paternal roof for some little time, was living bachelorwise, in Furnival's Inn. What was his astonish. ment, when Mr. Hall came in, to find he was the same person who had sold him the copy of the magazine containing his first story—that memorable copy at which he had looked, in Westminster Hall, through eyes bedimmed with joyful tears. Such coincidences always had for Dickens a peculiar, almost a superstitious, interest. The circumstance seemed of happy augury to both the "high contracting parties." Publisher and author were for the nonce on the best of terms. The latter, no doubt, saw his opening; was more than ready to undertake the work, and had no quarrel with the remuneration offered. But even then he was not the man to play second fiddle to anybody. Before they parted, he had quite succeeded in turning the tables on Seymour. The original proposal had been that the artist should produce four caricatures on sporting subjects every month, and that the letter-press should be in illustration of the caricatures. Dickens got Mr. Hall to agree to reverse that position. *He*, Dickens, was to have the command of the story, and the artist was to illustrate *him*. How far these altered relations would have worked quite smoothly if Seymour had lived, and if Dickens' story had not so soon assumed the proportions of a colossal success, it is idle to speculate. Seymour died by his own hand before the second number was published, and so ceased to be in a position to assert himself. It was, however, in deference to the peculiar bent of his art that Mr. Winkle, with his disastrous sporting proclivities, made part of the first conception of the book; and it is also very significant of the book's origin, that the design on the green wrapper in which the monthly parts made their appearance, should have had a purely sporting character, and exhibited Mr. Pickwick sleepily fishing in a punt, and Mr. Winkle shooting at what looks like a cock-sparrow,—

the whole surrounded by a chaste arabesque of guns, rods, and landing-nets. To Seymour, too, we owe the portrait of Mr. Pickwick, which has impressed that excellent old gentleman's face and figure upon all our memories. But to return to Dickens' interview with Mr. Hall. They seem to have parted in mutual satisfaction. At least it is certain Dickens was satisfied, for in a letter written, apparently on the same day, to " my dearest Kate," he thus sums up the proposals of the publishers : " They have made me an offer of fourteen pounds a month to write and edit a new publication they contemplate, entirely by myself, to be published monthly, and each number to contain four wood-cuts. . . . The work will be no joke, but the emolument is too tempting to resist." [1]

So, little thinking how soon he would begin to regard the " emolument " as ludicrously inadequate, he set to work on " Pickwick." The first part was published on the 31st of March or 1st of April, 1836.

That part seems scarcely to have created any sensation. Mr James Grant, the novelist, says indeed, that the first five parts were " a dead failure," and that the publishers were even debating whether the enterprise had not better be abandoned altogether, when suddenly Sam Weller appeared upon the scene, and turned their gloom into laughter. Be that as it may, certain it is that before many months had passed, Messrs. Chapman and Hall must have been thoroughly confirmed in a policy of perseverance. " The first order for Part I.," that is, the first order for binding, " was," says the bookbinder who executed the work, " for four hundred copies

[1] See the Letters published by Chapman and Hall.

only." The order for Part XV. had risen to forty thousand. All contemporary accounts agree that the success was sudden, immense. The author, like Lord Byron, some twenty-five years before, "awoke and found himself famous." Young as he was, not having yet numbered more than twenty-four summers, he at one stride reached the topmost height of popularity. Everybody read his book. Everybody laughed over it. Everybody talked about it. Everybody felt, confusedly perhaps, but very surely, that a new and vital force had arisen in English literature.

And English literature just then was in one of its times of slackness, rather than full flow. The great tide of the beginning of the century had ebbed. The tide of the Victorian age had scarcely begun to do more than ripple and flash on the horizon. Byron was dead, and Shelley and Keats and Coleridge and Lamb; Southey's life was on the decline; Wordsworth had long executed his best work; while of the coming men, Carlyle, though in the plenitude of his power, having published "Sartor Resartus," had not yet published his "French Revolution," [1] or delivered his lectures on the "Heroes," and was not yet in the plenitude of his fame and influence; and Macaulay, then in India, was known only as the essayist and politician; and Lord Tennyson and the Brownings were more or less names of the future. Looking especially at fiction, the time may be said to have been waiting for its master-novelist. Five years had gone by since the good and great Sir Walter Scott had been laid to rest in Dryburgh Abbey,

[1] It was finished in January, 1837, and not published till six months afterwards.

there to sleep, as is most fit, amid the ruins of that old Middle Age world he loved so well, with the babble of the Tweed for lullaby. Nor had any one shown himself of stature to step into his vacant place, albeit Bulwer, more precocious even than Dickens, was already known as the author of "Pelham," "Eugene Aram," and the "Last Days of Pompeii;" and Disraeli had written "Vivian Grey," and his earlier books; while Thackeray, Charlotte Brontë, Kingsley, George Eliot were all, of course, to come later. No, there was a vacant throne among the novelists. Here was the hour—and here, too, was the man. In virtue of natural kingship he took up his sceptre unquestioned.

Still, it may not be superfluous to inquire into the why and wherefore of his success. All effects have a cause. What was the cause of this special phenomenon? In the first place, the admirable freshness of the book won its way into every heart. There is a fervour of youth and healthy good spirits about the whole thing. In a former generation, Byron had uttered his wail of despair over a worthless world. We, in our own time, have got back to the dreary point of considering whether life be worth living. Here was a writer who had no such misgivings. For him life was pleasant, useful, full of delight—to be not only tolerated, but enjoyed. He liked its sights, its play of character, its adventures—affected no superiority to its amusements and convivialities—thoroughly laid himself out to please and to be pleased. And his characters were in the same mood. Their fund of animal spirits seemed inexhaustible. For life's jollities they were never unprepared. No doubt there were

"mighty mean moments" in their existence, as there
have been in the existence of most of us. It cannot have
been pleasant to Mr. Winkle to have his eye blackened
by the obstreperous cabman. Mr. Tracy Tupman probably felt a passing pang when jilted by the maiden aunt
in favour of the audacious Jingle. No man would elect
to occupy the position of defendant in an action for
breach of promise, or prefer to sojourn in a debtors'
prison. But how jauntily do Mr. Pickwick and his
friends shake off such discomforts ! How buoyantly do
they override the billows that beset their course ! And
what excellent digestions they have, and how slightly do
they seem to suffer the next day from any little excesses
in the matter of milk punch !

Then besides the good spirits and good temper, there
is Dickens' royal gift of humour. As some actors have
only to show their face and utter a word or two, in order
to convulse an audience with merriment, so here does
almost every sentence hold good and honest laughter.
Not, perhaps, objects the superfine and too dainty critic,
humour of the most delicate sort—not humour that for
its rare and exquisite quality can be placed beside the
masterpieces in that kind of Lamb, or Sterne, or Goldsmith, or Washington Irving. Granted freely ; not humour
of that special character. But very good humour nevertheless, the thoroughly popular humour of broad comedy
and obvious farce—the humour that finds its account
where absurd characters are placed in ridiculous situations,
that delights in the oddities of the whimsical and eccentric,
that irradiates stupidity and makes dulness amusing. How
thoroughly wholesome it is too ! To be at the same time

merry and wise, says the old adage, is a hard combination. Dickens was both. With all his boisterous merriment, his volleys of inextinguishable laughter, he never makes game of what is at all worthy of respect. Here, as in his later books, right is right, and wrong wrong, and he is never tempted to jingle his jester's bell out of season, and make right look ridiculous. And if the humour of " Pickwick " be wholesome, it is also most genial and kindly. We have here no acrid cynic sneeringly pointing out the plague spots of humanity, and showing pleasantly how even the good are tainted with evil. Rather does Dickens delight in finding some touch of goodness, some lingering memory of better things, some hopeful aspiration, some trace of unselfish devotion in characters where all seems soddened and lost. In brief, the laughter is the laughter of one who sees the foibles, and even the vices of his fellow-men, and yet looks on them lovingly and helpfully.

So much the first readers of " Pickwick " might note as the book unfolded itself to them, part by part; and they might also note one or two things besides. They might note—they could scarcely fail to do so—that though there was a touch of caricature in nearly all the characters, yet those characters were, one and all, wonderfully real, and very much alive. It was no world of shadows to which the author introduced them. Mr. Pickwick had a very distinct existence, and so had his three friends, and Bob Sawyer, and Benjamin Allen, and Mr. Jingle, and Tony Weller, and all the swarm of minor characters. While as to Sam Weller, if it be really true that he averted impending ruin from the book, and turned defeat into victory, one can only say that it was like him. When did he ever "stint stroke" in "foughten field"? By what array of adverse circumstances was he ever taken at a disadvantage? To have created a character of this vitality, of this individual force, would be a feather in the cap of any novelist who ever lived. Something I think of Dickens' own blood passed into this special progeniture of his. It has been irreverently said that Falstaff might represent Shakespeare in his cups, just as Hamlet might represent him in his more sober moments. So I have always had a kind of fancy that Sam Weller might be regarded as Dickens himself seen in a certain aspect—a sort of Dickens, shall I say?—in an humbler sphere of life, and who had never devoted himself to literature. There is in both the same energy, pluck, essential goodness of heart, fertility of resource, abundance of animal spirits, and also an imagination of a peculiar kind, in which wit enters as a main ingredient. And having noted how highly vitalized were the characters in "Pickwick," I think the first readers might also fairly be expected to note,—and, in fact, it is clear from Dickens' preface that they did note—how greatly the book increased in scope and power as it proceeded. The beginning was conceived almost in a spirit of farce. The incidents and adventures had scarcely any other object than to create amusement. Mr. Pickwick himself appeared on the scene with fantastic honours and the badge of absurdity, as "the man who had traced to their source the mighty ponds of Hampstead, and agitated the scientific world with the Theory of Tittlebats." But in all this there is a gradual change. Mr. Pickwick is presented to us latterly as an exceedingly sound-headed as well as sound-hearted old gentleman, whom we should never think of associating with the sources of Hampstead Ponds or any other folly. While in such scenes as those at the Fleet Prison, the author is clearly endeavouring to do much more than raise a laugh. He is sounding the deeper, more tragic chords in human feeling

Ah, if we add to all this—to the freshness, the "go," the good spirits, the keen observation, the graphic painting, the humour, the vitality of the characters, the gradual development of power—if we add to all this that something which is in all, and greater than all, viz., genius, and genius of a highly popular kind, then we shall have no difficulty in understanding why everybody read " Pickwick," and how it came to pass that its publishers made some £20,000 by a work that they had once thought of abandoning as worthless.[1]

[1] They acknowledged to Dickens that they had made £14,000 by the sale of the monthly parts alone.

CHAPTER IV.

D ICKENS was not at all the man to rest on his oars
while " Pickwick " was giving such a magnificent
impetus to the boat that contained his fortunes. The
amount of work which he accomplished in the years
1836, 1837, 1838, and 1839 is, if we consider its quality,
amazing. " Pickwick," as we have seen, was begun with
the first of these years, and its publication continued
till the November of 1837. Independently of his work
on " Pickwick," he was, in the year 1836, engaged in the
arduous profession of a reporter till the close of the
parliamentary session, and also wrote a pamphlet on
Sabbatarianism, a farce in two acts, " The Strange
Gentleman," for the St. James's Theatre, and a comic
opera, " The Village Coquettes," which was set to music
by Hullah. With the very commencement of 1837—
" Pickwick," it will be remembered, going on all the
while—he entered upon the duties of editor of
Bentley's Miscellany, and in the second number began
the publication of " Oliver Twist," which was continued
into the early months of 1839, when his connection
with the magazine ceased. In the April of 1838, and
simultaneously, of course, with " Oliver Twist," appeared

4

the first part of "Nicholas Nickleby"—the last part appearing in the October of the following year. Three novels of more than full size and of first-rate importance, in less than four years, besides a good deal of other miscellaneous work—certainly that was "good going." The pace was decidedly fast. Small wonder that *The Quarterly Review*, even so early as October, 1837, was tempted to croak about "Mr. Dickens" as writing "too often and too fast, and putting forth in their crude, unfinished, undigested state, thoughts, feelings, observations, and plans which it required time and study to mature," and to warn him that as he had "risen like a rocket," so he was in danger of "coming down like the stick." Small wonder, I say, and yet to us now, how unjust the accusation appears, and how false the prophecy. Rapidly as those books were executed, Dickens, like the real artist that he was, had put into them his best work. There was no scamping. The critics of the time judged superficially, not making allowance for the ample fund of observations he had amassed, for the genuine fecundity of his genius, and for the admirable industry of an extremely industrious man. "The World's Workers"—there exists under that general designation a series of short biographies, for which Miss Dickens has written a sketch of her father's life. To no one could the description more fittingly apply. Throughout his life he worked desperately hard. He possessed, in a high degree, the "infinite faculty for taking pains," which is so great an adjunct to genius, though it is not, as the good Sir Joshua Reynolds held, genius itself. Thus what he had done rapidly was done well; and, for the rest, the writer, who had yet to give the world "Martin Chuzzlewit," "The Christmas Carol," "David Copperfield," and "Dombey," was not "coming down like a stick." There were many more stars, and of very brilliant colours, to be showered out by that rocket; and the stick has not even yet fallen to the ground.[1]

Naturally, with the success of "Pickwick," came a great change in Dickens' pecuniary position. He had, as we have seen, been glad enough, before he began the book, to close with the offer of £14 for each monthly part. That sum was afterwards increased to £15, and the two first payments seem to have been made in advance for the purpose of helping him to defray the expenses of his marriage. But as the sale leapt up, the publishers themselves felt that such a rate of re-muneration was altogether insufficient, and sent him, first and last, a goodly number of supplementary cheques, for sums amounting in the aggregate, as *they* computed, to £3,000, and as Forster computes to about £2,500. This Dickens, who, to use his own words, "never undervalued his own work," considered a very inadequate percentage on their gains—forgetting a little, perhaps, that the risks had been wholly theirs, and that he had been more than content with the original bargain. Similarly he was soon utterly dissatisfied with his arrangements with Bentley about the editorship of the *Miscellany* and "Oliver Twist,"—arrangements which had been

---

[1] I think critics, and perhaps I myself, have been a little hard on this Quarterly Reviewer. He did not, after all, say that Dickens would come down like a stick, only that he might do so if he wrote too fast and furiously.

entered into in August, 1836, while " Pickwick " was in
progress; and he utterly refused to let that publisher
have " Gabriel Varden, The Locksmith of London "
(" Barnaby Rudge") on the terms originally agreed upon.
With Macrone also, who had made some £4,000 by the
"Sketches," and given him about £400, he was no
better pleased, especially when that enterprising gentleman threatened a re-issue in monthly parts, and so
compelled him to re-purchase the copyright for £2,000.
But however much he might consider himself ill-treated
by the publishing fraternity, he was, of course, rapidly
getting far richer than he had been, and so able to
enlarge his mode of life.   He had begun, modestly
enough, by taking his wife to live with him in his
bachelor's quarters in Furnival's Inn,—much as Tommy
Traddles, in " David Copperfield," took *his* wife to live
in chambers at Gray's Inn; and there, in Furnival's Inn,
his first child, a boy, was born on the 6th of January,
1837.   But in the March of that year he moved to a more
commodious dwelling, at 48, Doughty Street, where he
remained till the end of 1839, when still increasing
means enabled him to move to a still better house at
1, Devonshire Terrace, Regent's Park.   But the house
in Doughty Street must have been endeared to him
by many memories.   It was there, on the 7th of
May, 1837, that he lost, at the early age of seventeen,
and quite suddenly, a sister-in-law, Mary Hogarth, to
whom he was greatly attached.   The blow fell so
heavily at the time as to incapacitate him from all
work, and delayed the publication of one of the numbers
of " Pickwick."   Nor was the sorrow only sharp and

transient. He speaks of her in the preface to the first
edition of that book. Her spirit seemed to be hovering
near as he stood looking at Niagara. He felt her
hallowing influence when in danger of growing too
much elated by his first reception in America. She
came back to him in dreams in Italy. Her image
remained in his heart, unchanged by time, as he declared,
to the very end. She represented to his mind all that
was pure and lovely in opening womanhood, and
lives, in the world created by his art, as the Little
Nell of "The Old Curiosity Shop." It was in
Doughty Street, too, that he began to gather round
him the circle of friends whose names seem almost
like a muster-roll of the famous men and women in the
first thirty years of Queen Victoria's reign. I shall not
enumerate them. The list of writers, artists, actors,
would be too long. But this at least it would be unjust
not to note, that among his friends were included nearly
all those who by any stretch of fancy could be regarded
as his rivals in the fields of humour and fiction. With
Washington Irving, Hood, Douglas Jerrold, Lord Lytton,
Harrison Ainsworth, Mr. Wilkie Collins, Mrs. Gaskell,
and, save for a passing foolish quarrel, with Thackeray,
the novelist who really was his peer, he maintained
the kindliest and most cordial relations. Nor when
George Eliot published her first books, "The Scenes
of Clerical Life" and "Adam Bede," did any one
acknowledge their excellence more freely. Petty
jealousies found no place in the nature of this great
writer.

It was also while living at Doughty Street that he

seems, in great measure, to have formed those habits of
work and relaxation which every artist fashions so as to
suit his own special needs and idiosyncrasies. His
favourite time for work was the morning, between the
hours of breakfast and lunch; and though, at this particular period, the enormous pressure of his engagements
compelled him to work "double tides," and often far
into the night, yet he was essentially a day-worker, not
a night-worker. Like the great German poet Goethe,
he preferred to exercise his art in the fresh morning
hours, when the dewdrops, as it were, lay bright upon
his imagination and fancy. And for relaxation and
sedative, when he had thoroughly worn himself out
with mental toil, he would have recourse to the
hardest bodily exercise. At first riding seems to have
contented him—fifteen miles out and fifteen miles in,
with a halt at some road-side inn for refreshment.
But soon walking took the place of riding, and he
became an indefatigable pedestrian. He would think
nothing of a walk of twenty or thirty miles, and that
not merely in the vigorous heyday of youth, but afterwards, to the very last. He was always on those alert,
quick feet of his, perambulating London from end to end,
and in every direction; perambulating the suburbs, perambulating the "greater London" that lies within a
radius of twenty miles, round the central core of metro-
politan houses. In short, he was everywhere, in all
weathers, at all hours. Nor was London, smaller and
greater, his only walking field. He would walk wherever
he was—walked through and through Genoa, and all
about Genoa, when he lived there; knew every inch of

the Kent country round Broadstairs and round Gad's
Hill—was, as I have said, always, always, always on his
feet. But if he would pedestrianize everywhere, London
remained the walking ground of his heart. As Dr.
Johnson held that nothing equalled a stroll down Fleet
Street, so did Dickens, sitting in full view of Genoa's
perfect bay, and with the blue Mediterranean sparkling
at his feet, turn in thought for inspiration to his old
haunts. "Never," he writes to Forster, when about to
begin "The Chimes," "never did I stagger so upon a
threshold before. I seem as if I had plucked myself out
of my proper soil when I left Devonshire Terrace, and
could take root no more until I return to it. . . . Did I
tell you how many fountains we have here? No matter.
If they played nectar, they wouldn't please me half so
well as the West Middlesex Waterworks at Devonshire
Terrace. . . Put me down on Waterloo Bridge at eight
o'clock in the evening, with leave to roam about as long
as I like, and I would come home, as you know, panting
to go on. I am sadly strange as it is, and can't settle."
"Eight o'clock in the evening,"—that points to another of his peculiarities. As he liked best to walk in
London, so he liked best to walk at night. The darkness of the great city had a strange fascination for him.
He never grew tired of it, would find pleasure and
refreshment, when most weary and jaded, in losing
himself in it, in abandoning himself to its mysteries.
Looked at with this knowledge, the opening of the "Old
Curiosity Shop" becomes a passage of autobiography.
And how all these wanderings must have served him in
his art! Remember what a keen observer he was, per-

haps one of the keenest that ever lived, and then think what food for observation he would thus be constantly collecting.   To the eye that knows how to see, there is no stage where so many scenes from the drama of life are being always enacted as the streets of London. Dickens frequented that theatre very assiduously, and of his power of sight there can be no question.

CHAPTER V.

"PICKWICK" had been a novel without any plot. The story, if story it can be called, bore every trace of its hasty origin. Scene succeeded scene, and incident incident, and Mr. Pickwick and his three friends were hurried about from place to place, and through adventures of all kinds, without any particularly defined purpose. In truth, many people, and myself among the number, find some difficulty in reading the book as a connected narrative, and prefer to take it piecemeal. But in "Oliver Twist" there is a serious effort to work out a coherent plot, and real unity of conception. Whether that conception be based on probability, is another point. Oliver is the illegitimate son of a young lady who has lapsed from virtue under circumstances of great temptation, but still lapsed from virtue, and who dies in giving him birth. He is brought up as a pauper child in a particularly ill-managed workhouse, and apprenticed to a low undertaker. Thence he escapes, and walks to London, where he falls in with a gang of thieves. His legitimate brother, an unutterable scoundrel, happens to see him in London, and recognizing him by a likeness to their common father, bribes the thieves to recapture him when he has escaped from their clutches. Now I would rather not say whether I consider it quite likely that a boy of this birth and nurture would fly at a boy much bigger than himself in vindication of the fair fame of a mother whom he had never known, or would freely risk his life to warn a sleeping household that they were being robbed, or would, on all occasions, exhibit the most excellent manners and morals, and a delicacy of feeling that is quite dainty. But this is the essence of the book. To show purity and goodness of disposition as self-sufficient in themselves to resist all adverse influences, is Dickens' main object. Take Oliver's sweet uncontaminated character away, and the story crumbles to pieces. With mere improbabilities of plot, I have no quarrel. Of course it is not likely that the boy, on the occasion of his first escape from the thieves, should be rescued by his father's oldest friend, and, on the second occasion, come across his aunt. But such coincidences must be accepted in any story; they violate no truth of character. I am afraid I can't say as much of Master Oliver's graces and virtues.

With this reservation, however, how much there is in the book to which unstinted admiration can be given! As "Pickwick" first fully exhibited the humorous side of Dickens' genius, so "Oliver Twist" first fully exhibited its tragic side;—the pathetic side was to come somewhat later. The scenes at the workhouse; at the thieves' dens in London; the burglary; the murder of poor Nancy; the escape and death of the horror-haunted Sikes,—all are painted with a master's hand. And the book, like its predecessor, and like those that were to follow, contains characters that have passed into common knowledge as types,—characters of the keenest individu- ' ality, and that yet seem in themselves to sum up a whole class. Such are Bill Sikes, whose ruffianism has an almost epic grandeur ; and black-hearted Fagin, the Jew, receiver of stolen goods and trainer of youth in the way they should *not* go ; and Master Dawkins, the Artful Dodger. Such, too, is Mr. Bumble, greatest and most unhappy of beadles.

Comedy had predominated in " Pickwick," tragedy in " Oliver Twist." The more complete fusion of the two was effected in " Nicholas Nickleby." But as the mighty actor Garrick, in the well-known picture by Sir Joshua Reynolds, is drawn towards the more mirthful of the two sisters, so, here again, I think that comedy decidedly bears away the palm,—though tragedy is not beaten altogether without a struggle either. Here is the story as it unfolds itself. The two heroes are Ralph Nickleby and his nephew Nicholas. They stand forth, almost from the beginning, as antagc ists, in battle array the one against the other ; and the story is, in the main, a history of the campaigns between them — cunning and greed being mustered on the one side, and young, generous courage on the other. At first Nicholas believes in his uncle, who promises to befriend Nicholas's mother and sister, and obtains for Nicholas himself a situation as usher in a Yorkshire school kept by one Squeers. But the young fellow's gorge rises at the sickening cruelty exercised in the school, and he leaves it, having first beaten Mr. Squeers,—leaves it followed by a poor shattered creature called Smike. Meanwhile Ralph, the usurer, befriends

his sister-in-law and niece after his own fashion, and tries
to use the latter's beauty in furtherance of his trade as a
money-lender.   Nicholas discovers his plots, frustrates all
his schemes, rescues, and ultimately marries, a young
lady who had been immeshed in one of them; and
Ralph, at last, utterly beaten, commits suicide on finding
that Smike, through whom he had been endeavouring all
through to injure Nicholas, and who is now dead, was his
own son.   Such are the book's dry bones, its skeleton,
which one is almost ashamed to expose thus nakedly.
For the beauty of these novels lies not at all in the plot;
it is in the incidents, situations, characters.   And with
beauty of this kind how richly dowered is "Nicholas
Nickleby"!   Take the characters alone.   What lavish
profusion of humour in the theatrical group that clusters
round Mr. Vincent Crumules, the country manager; and
in the Squeers family too; and in the little shop-world of
Mrs. Mantalini, the fashionable dressmaker; and in
Cheerible Brothers, the golden-hearted old merchants
who take Nicholas into their counting-house.   Then for
single characters commend me to Mrs. Nickleby, whose
logic, which some cynics would call feminine, is positively
sublime in its want of coherence; and to John Browdie,
the honest Yorkshire cornfactor, as good a fellow almost
as Dandie Dimnont, the Border yeoman whom Scott
made immortal.   The high-life personages are far less
successful.   Dickens had small gift that way, and seldom
succeeded in his society pictures.   Nor, if the truth must
be told, do I greatly care for the description of the duel
between Sir Mulberry Hawk and Lord Verisopht, though
it was evidently very much admired at the time, and is

quoted, as a favourable specimen of Dickens' style, in Charles Knight's "Half-hours with the Best Authors." The writing is a little too *tall*. It lacks simplicity, as is sometimes the case with Dickens, when he wants to be particularly impressive.

And this leads me, by a kind of natural sequence, to what I have to say about his next book, "The Old Curiosity Shop;" for here, again, though in a very much more marked degree, I fear I shall have to run counter to a popular opinion.

But first a word as to the circumstances under which the book was published. Casting about, after the conclusion of "Nicholas Nickleby," for further literary ventures, Dickens came to the conclusion that the public must be getting tired of his stories in monthly parts. It occurred to him that a weekly periodical, somewhat after the manner of Addison's *Spectator* or Goldsmith's *Bee*, and containing essays, stories, and miscellaneous papers, —to be written mainly, but not entirely, by himself,— would be just the thing to revive interest, and give his popularity a spur. Accordingly an arrangement was entered into with Messrs. Chapman and Hall, by which they covenanted to give him £50 for each weekly number of such a periodical, and half profits; —and the first number of *Master Humphrey's Clock* made its appearance in the April of 1840. Unfortunately Dickens had reckoned altogether without his host. The public were not to be cajoled. What they expected from their favourite was novels, not essays, short stories, or sketches, however admirable. The orders for the first number had amounted to seventy

thousand; but they fell off as soon as it was discovered
that Master Humphrey, sitting by his clock, had no
intention of beguiling the world with a continuous
narrative,—that the title, in short, did not stand for
the title of a novel.   Either the times were not ripe for
the *Household Words*, which, ten years afterwards, proved
to be such a great and permanent success, or Dickens
had laid his plans badly.   Vainly did he put forth
all his powers, vainly did he bring back upon the stage
those old popular favourites, Mr. Pickwick, Sam Weller,
and Tony Weller.   All was of no avail.   Clearly, in order
to avoid defeat, a change of front had become necessary.
The novel of " The Old Curiosity Shop " was accordingly
commenced in the fourth number of the *Clock*, and very
soon acted the cuckoo's part of thrusting Master
Humphrey and all that belonged to him out of the nest.
He disappeared pretty well from the periodical, and
when the novel was republished, the whole machinery
of the *Clock* had gone ;—and with it I may add, some
very characteristic and admirable writing.   Dickens
himself confessed that he "winced a little," when
the "opening paper, . . . in which Master Humphrey
described himself and his manner of life," "became
the property of the trunkmaker and the butterman ;"
and most Dickens lovers will agree with me in rejoicing
that the omitted parts have now at last been tardily rescued from unmerited neglect, and finds a place in the
recently issued " Charles Dickens " edition of the works.

There is no hero in " The Old Curiosity Shop,"—unless
Mr. Richard Swiveller, "perpetual grand-master of the
Glorious Apollos," be the questionable hero ; and the

heroine is Little Nell, a child. Of Dickens' singular feeling for the pathos and humour of childhood, I have already spoken. Many novelists, perhaps one might even say, most novelists, have no freedom of utterance when they come to speak about children, do not know what to do with a child if it chances to stray into their pages. But how different with Dickens! He is never more thoroughly at home than with the little folk. Perhaps his best speech, and they all are good, is the one uttered at the dinner given on behalf of the Children's Hospital. Certainly there is no figure in "Dombey and Son" on which more loving care has been lavished than the figure of little Paul, and when the lad dies one quite feels that the light has gone out of the book. "David Copperfield" shorn of David's childhood and youth would be a far less admirable performance. The hero of "Oliver Twist" is a boy. Pip is a boy through a fair portion of "Great Expectations." The heroine of "The Old Curiosity Shop" is, as I have just said, a girl. And of all these children, the one who seems, from the first, to have stood highest in popular favour, and won most hearts, is Little Nell. Ay me, what tears have been shed over her weary wanderings with that absurd old gambling grandfather of hers; how many persons have sorrowed over her untimely end as if she had been a daughter or a sister. High and low, literate and illiterate, over nearly all has she cast her spell. Hood, he who sang the "Song of the Shirt," paid her the tribute of his admiration, and Jeffrey, the hard-headed old judge and editor of *The Edinburgh Review*, the tribute of his tears.

Landor volleyed forth his thunderous praises over her grave, likening her to Juliet and Desdemona. Nay, Dickens himself sadly bewailed her fate, described himself as being the "wretchedest of the wretched" when it drew near, and shut himself from all society as if he had suffered a real bereavement. While as to the feeling which she has excited in the breasts of the illiterate, we may take Mr. Bret Harte's account of the haggard golddiggers by the roaring Californian camp fire, who throw down their cards to listen to her story, and, for the nonce, are softened and humanized.[1]—Such is the sympathy she has created. And for the description of her death and burial, as a superb piece of pathetic writing, there has been a perfect chorus of praise broken here and there no doubt by a discordant voice, but still of the loudest and most heartfelt. Did not Horne, a poet better known to the last generation than to this, point out that though printed as prose, these passages were, perhaps as "the result of harmonious accident," essentially poetry, and "written in blank verse of irregular metres and rhythms, which Southey and Shelley and some other poets have occasionally adopted"? Did he not print part of the passages in this form, substituting only, as a concession to the conventionalities of verse, the word "grandames" for "grandmothers"; and did he not declare of one of the extracts so printed that it was "worthy of the best passages in Wordsworth"?

If it "argues an insensibility" to stand somewhat unmoved among all these tears and admiration, I am afraid I must be rather pebble-hearted. To tell the

[1] "Dickens in Camp."

whole damaging truth, I am, and always have been,
only slightly affected by the story of Little Nell; have
never felt any particular inclination to shed a tear over
it, and consider the closing chapters as failing of their
due effect, on me at least, because they are pitched in
a key that is altogether too high and unnatural. Of
course one makes a confession of this kind with
diffidence. It is no light thing to stem the current of a
popular opinion. But one can only go with the stream
when one thinks the stream is flowing in a right channel.
And here I think the stream is meandering out of its
course. For me, Little Nell is scarcely more than a
figure in cloudland. Possibly part of the reason why I
do not feel as much sympathy with her as I ought, is
because I do not seem to know her very well. With
Paul Dombey I am intimately acquainted. I should
recognize the child anywhere, should be on the
best of terms with him in five minutes. Few things
would give me greater pleasure than an hour's saunter
by the side of his little invalid's carriage along the
Parade at Brighton. How we should laugh, to be sure,
if we happened to come across Mr. Toots, and smile,
too, if we met Feeder, B.A., and give a furtive glance
of recognition at Glubb, the discarded charioteer. Then
the classic Cornelia Blimber would pass, on her
constitutional, and we should quail a little—at least I
am certain *I* should—as she bent upon us her scholastic
spectacles ; and a glimpse of Dr. Blimber would chill us
even more ; till—ah ! what's this ? Why does a flush of
happiness mantle over my little friend's pale face ? Why
does he utter a faint cry of pleasure ? Yes, there she is

5

—he has caught sight of Floy running forward to meet
him.—So am I led, almost instinctively, whenever the
figure of Paul flashes into my mind, to think of him as
a child I have actually known. But Nell—she has no
such reality of existence. She has been etherealized,
vapourized, rhapsodized about, till the flesh and blood
have gone out of her. I recognize her attributes,
unselfishness, sweetness of disposition, gentleness. But
these don't constitute a human being.. They don't make
up a recognizable individuality. If I met her in the
street, I am afraid I should not know her; and if I did,
I am sure we should both find it difficult to keep up a
conversation.

Do the passages describing her death and burial
really possess the rhythm of poetry? That would
seem to me, I confess, to be as ill a compliment as to
say of a piece of poetry that it was really prose. The
music of prose and of poetry are essentially different.
They do not affect the ear in the same way. The one
is akin to song, the other to speech. Give to prose
the recurring cadences, the measure, and the rhythmic
march of verse, and it becomes bad prose without
becoming good poetry.[1] So, in fairness to Dickens, one
is bound, as far as one can, to forget Horne's misapplied
praise. But even thus, and looking upon it as prose
alone, can we say that the account of Nell's funeral is, in
the high artistic sense, a piece of good work. Here is
an extract: "And now the bell—the bell she had so
often heard, by night and day, and listened to with

[1] Dickens himself knew that he had a tendency to fall into blank
verse in moments of excitement, and tried to guard against it,

solemn pleasure almost as a living voice—rang its remorseless toll, for her, so young, so beautiful, so good. Decrepit age, and vigorous life, and blooming youth, and helpless infancy, poured forth—on crutches, in the pride of strength and health, in the full blush of promise, in the mere dawn of life—to gather round her tomb. Old men were there, whose eyes were dim and senses failing—grandmothers, who might have died ten years ago, and still been old,—the deaf, the blind, the lame, the palsied, the living dead in many shapes and forms, to see the closing of that earthly grave. What was the death it would shut in, to that which still could crawl and creep above it ? " Such is the tone throughout, and one feels inclined to ask whether it is quite the appropriate tone in which to speak of the funeral of a child in a country churchyard ? All this pomp of rhetoric seems to me—shall I say it ?—as much out of place as if Nell had been buried like some great soldier or minister of state—with a hearse, all sable velvet and nodding plumes, drawn by a long train of sable steeds, and a final discharge of artillery over the grave. The verbal honours paid here to the deceased are really not much less incongruous and out of keeping. Surely in such a subject, above all others, the pathos of simplicity would have been most effective.

There are some, indeed, who deny to Dickens the gift of pathos altogether. Such persons acknowledge, for the most part a little unwillingly, that he was a master of humour of the broader, more obvious kind. But they assert that all his sentiment is mawkish and overstrained, and that his efforts to compel our tears are so obvious as to defeat their own purpose. Now it will be clear, from what I have said about Little Nell, that I am capable of appreciating the force of any criticism of this kind; nay, that I go so far as to acknowledge that Dickens occasionally lays himself open to it. But go one inch beyond this I cannot. Of course we may, if we like, take up a position of pure stoicism, and deny pathos altogether, in life as in art. We may regard all human affairs but as a mere struggle for existence, and say that might makes right, and that the weak is only treated according to his deserts when he goes to the wall. We may hold that neither sorrow nor suffering call for any meed of sympathy. Such is mainly the attitude which the French novelist adopts towards the world of his creation.[1] But once admit that feeling is legitimate; once allow that tears are due to those who have been crushed and left bleeding by this great world of ours as it crashes blundering on its way; once grant that the writer's art can properly embrace what Shakespeare calls " the pity of it," the sorrows inwoven in all our human relationships; once acknowledge all this, and then I affirm, most confidently, that Dickens, working at his best, was one of the greatest masters of pathos who ever lived. I can myself see scarce a strained discordant note in the account of the short life and early death of Paul Dombey, and none in the description of the death of Paul Dombey's mother, or in the story of Tiny Tim, or in the record of David Copperfield's childhood and boyhood. I consider the passage in "American Notes" describing the traits of gentle kindliness among the emigrants as

[1] M. Daudet, in many respects a follower of Dickens, is a fine and notable exception.

being nobly, pathetically eloquent. Did space allow, I could support my position by quotations and example to any extent. And my conclusion is that, though he failed with Little Nell, yet he succeeded elsewhere, and superbly.

The number of *Master Humphrey's Clock*, containing the conclusion of "The Old Curiosity Shop," appeared on the 17th of January, 1841, and "Barnaby Rudge" began its course in the ensuing week. The first had been essentially a tale of modern life. All the characters that made a kind of background, mostly grotesque or hideous, for the figure of Little Nell, were characters of to-day, or at least of the day when the book was written ; for I must not forget that that day ran into the past some six and forty years ago. Quilp, the dwarf,—and a far finer specimen of a scoundrel by the by, in every respect, than that poor stage villain Monks ; Sampson Brass and his legal sister Sally, a goodly pair ; Kit, golden-hearted and plain of body, who so barely escapes from the plot laid by the afore-mentioned worthies to prove him a thief ; Chuckster, most lady-killing of notaries' clerks ; Mrs. Jarley, the good-natured waxwork woman, in whose soul there would be naught save kindliness, only she cannot bring herself to tolerate Punch and Judy ; Short and Codlin, the Punch and Judy men ; the little misused servant, whom Dick Swiveller in his grandeur creates a marchioness ; and the magnificent Swiveller himself, prince among the idle and impecunious, justifying by his snatches of song, and flowery rhetoric, his high position as "perpetual grand-master" among the "Glorious Apollers,"—all these, making allowance perhaps for some idealization, were personages of Dickens' own time. But in "Barnaby Rudge,"

Dickens threw himself back into the last century. The book is a historical novel, one of the two which he wrote, the other being the "Tale of Two Cities," and its scenes are many of them laid among the No Popery Riots of 1780.

A ghastly time, a time of aimless, brutal incendiarism and mad turbulence on the part of the mob; a time of weakness and ineptitude on the part of the Government; a time of wickedness, folly, and misrule. Dickens describes it admirably. His picture of the riots themselves seems painted in pigments of blood and fire; and yet, through all the hurry and confusion, he retains the clearness of arrangement and lucidity which characterize the pictures of such subjects when executed by the great masters of the art—as Carlyle, for example. His portrait of the poor, crazy-brained creature, Lord George Gordon, who sowed the wind which the country was to reap in whirlwind, is excellent. Nor is what may be called the private part of the story unskilfully woven with the historical part. The plot, though not good, rises perhaps above the average of Dickens' plots ; for even we, his admirers, are scarcely bound to maintain that plot was his strong point. Beyond this, I think I may say that the book is, on the whole, the least characteristic of his books. It is the one which those who are most out of sympathy with his peculiar vein of humour and pathos will probably think the best, and the one which the true Dickens lovers will generally regard as bearing the greatest resemblance to an ordinary novel.

CHAPTER VI.

THE last number of " Barnaby Rudge " appeared in November, 1841, and, on the 4th of the following January Dickens sailed with his wife for a six months' tour in the United States. What induced him to undertake this journey, more formidable then, of course, than now ?

Mainly, I think, that restless desire to see the world which is strong in a great many men, and was specially strong in Dickens. Ride as he might, and walk as he might, his abounding energies remained unsatisfied. In 1837 there had been trips to Belgium, Broadstairs, Brighton ; in 1838 to Yorkshire, Broadstairs, North Wales, and a fairly long stay at Twickenham ; in 1839 a similar stay at Petersham — where, as at Twickenham, frolic gaiety and athletics had prevailed, —and trips to Broadstairs and Devonshire ; in 1840 trips again to Bath, Birmingham, Shakespeare's country, Broadstairs, Devonshire ; in 1841 more trips, and a very notable visit to Edinburgh, with which Little Nell had a great deal to do. For Lord Jeffrey was enamoured of that young lady, declaring to whomsoever

would hear that there had been "nothing so good
. . . since Cordelia ; " and inoculating the citizens
of the northern capital with his enthusiasm, he had
induced them to offer to Dickens a right royal banquet,
and the freedom of their city. Accordingly to Edinburgh
he repaired, and the dinner took place on the 26th of
June, with three hundred of the chief notabilities for enter-
tainers, and a reception such as kings might have envied.
Jeffrey himself was ill and unable to take the chair, but
Wilson, the leonine " Christopher North," editor of
Blackwood, and author of those "Noctes Ambrosianæ"
which were read so eagerly as they came out, and which
some of us find so difficult to read now—Wilson presided
most worthily. Of speechifying there was of course much,
and compliments abounded. But the banquet itself, the
whole reception at Edinburgh was the most magnificent
of compliments. Never, I imagine, can such efforts have
been made to turn any young man's brain, as were made,
during this and the following year, to turn the head of
Dickens, who was still, be it remembered, under thirty.
Nevertheless he came unscathed through the ordeal. A
kind of manly genuineness bore him through. Amid all
the adulation and excitement, the public and private
hospitalities, the semi-regal state appearance at the
theatre, he could write, and write truly, to his friend
Forster: "The moral of this is, that there is no place like
home ; and that I thank God most heartily for having
given me a quiet spirit and a heart that won't hold many
people. I sigh for Devonshire Terrace and Broadstairs,
for battledore and shuttlecock ; I want to dine in a
blouse with you and Mac (Maclise). . . . On Sunday

evening, the 17th July, I shall revisit my household gods,
please heaven. I wish the day were here."

Yes, except during the few years when he and his wife
lived unhappily together, he was greatly attached to his
home, with its friendships and simple pleasures ; but yet,
as I have said, a desire to see more of the world, and to
garner new experiences, was strong upon him. The two
conflicting influences often warred in his life, so that it
almost seemed sometimes as if he were being driven
by relentless furies. Those furies pointed now with
stern fingers towards America, though "how" he was
"to get on" "for seven or eight months without" his
friends, he could not upon his " soul conceive ;" though
he dreaded "to think of breaking up all " his "old happy
habits for so long a time ; " though " Kate," remembering
doubtless her four little children, wept whenever the
subject was "spoken of." Something made him feel
that the going was " a matter of imperative necessity."
Washington Irving beckoned from across the Atlantic,
speaking, as Jeffrey had spoken from Edinburgh, of
Little Nell and her far-extended influence. There was a
great reception foreshadowed, and a new world to be seen,
and a book to be written about it. While as to the
strongest of the home ties—the children that brought
the tears into Mrs. Dickens' eyes,—the separation, after
all, would not be eternal, and the good Macready, tragic
actor and true friend, would take charge of the little folk
while their parents were away. So Dickens, who had
some time before " begun counting the days between this
and coming home again," set sail, as I have said, for
America on the 4th of January, 1842.

And a very rough experience he, and Mrs. Dickens, and Mrs. Dickens' maid seem to have had during that January passage from Liverpool to Halifax and Boston. Most of the time it blew horribly, and they were direfully ill. Then a storm supervened, which swept away the paddle-boxes and stove in the life-boats, and they seem to have been in real peril. Next the ship struck on a mud-bank. But dangers and discomforts must have been forgotten, at any rate to begin with, in the glories of the reception that awaited the "inimitable,"—as Dickens whimsically called himself in those days,—when he landed in the New World. If he had been received with princely honours in Edinburgh, he was treated now as an emperor in some triumphant progress. Halifax sounded the first note of welcome, gave, as it were, the preliminary trumpet flourish. From that town he writes : " I wish you could have seen the crowds cheering the inimitable in the streets. I wish you could have seen judges, law-officers, bishops, and law-makers welcoming the inimitable. I wish you could have seen the inimitable shown to a great elbow-chair by the Speaker's throne, and sitting alone in the middle of the floor of the House of Commons, the observed of all observers, listening with exemplary gravity to the queerest speaking possible, and breaking, in spite of himself, into a smile as he thought of this commencement to the thousand and one stories in reserve for home." At Boston the enthusiasm had swelled to even greater proportions. "How can I give you," he writes, "the faintest notion of my reception here; of the crowds that pour in and out the whole day; of the people that line the streets when I

go out ; of the cheering when I went to the theatre ; of
the copies of verses, letters of congratulation, welcomes of
all kinds, balls, dinners, assemblies without end ? . . .
There is to be a dinner in New York, . . . to which I
have had an invitation with every known name in America
appended to it. . . . I have had deputations from the
Far West, who have come from more than two thousand
miles' distance ; from the lakes, the rivers, the backwoods,
the log-houses, the cities, factories, villages, and towns.
Authorities from nearly all the states have written to me.
I have heard from the universities, congress, senate, and
bodies, public and private, of every sort and kind." All
was indeed going happy as a marriage bell. Did I not
rightly say that the world was conspiring to spoil this
young man of thirty, whose youth had certainly not been
passed in the splendour of opulence or power ? What
wonder if in the dawn of his American experiences, and
of such a reception, everything assumed a roseate hue ?
Is it matter for surprise if he found the women "very
beautiful," the "general breeding neither stiff nor forward," "the good nature universal"; if he expatiated,
not without a backward look at unprogressive Old England, on the comparative comfort among the working
classes, and the absence of beggars in the streets ? But,
alas, that rosy dawn ended, as rosy dawns sometimes
will, in sleet and mist and very dirty weather. Before
many weeks, before many days had flown, Dickens was
writing in a very different spirit. On the 24th of February, in the midst of a perfect ovation of balls and dinners,
he writes " with reluctance, disappointment, and sorrow,"
that "there is no country on the face of the earth, where

there is less freedom of opinion on any subject in reference to which there is a broad difference of opinion, than in " the United States. On the 22nd of March he writes again, to Macready, who seems to have remonstrated with him on his growing discontent : "It is of no use, I *am* disappointed. This is not the republic I came to see ; this is not the republic of my imagination. I infinitely prefer a liberal monarchy—even with its sickening accompaniment of Court circulars—to such a government as this. The more I think of its youth and strength, the poorer and more trifling in a thousand aspects it appears in my eyes. In everything of which it has made a boast, excepting its education of the people, and its care for poor children, it sinks immeasurably below the level I had placed it upon, and England, even England, bad and faulty as the old land is, and miserable as millions of her people are, rises in the comparison. . . . Freedom of opinion ; where is it ? I see a press more mean and paltry and silly and disgraceful than any country I ever knew. . . . In the respects of not being left alone, and of being horribly disgusted by tobacco chewing and tobacco spittle, I have suffered considerably."

Extracts like these could be multiplied to any extent, and the question arises, why did such a change come over the spirit of Dickens ? Washington Irving, at the great New York dinner, had called him "the guest of the nation." Why was the guest so quickly dissatisfied with his host, and quarrelling with the character of his entertainment ? Sheer physical fatigue, I think, had a good deal to do with it. Even at

Boston, before he had begun to travel over the unending railways, water-courses, and chaotic coach-roads of the great Republic, that key-note had been sounded. "We are already," he had written, "weary at times, past all expression." Few men can wander with impunity out of their own professional sphere, and undertake duties for which they have neither the training nor acquired tastes. Dickens was a writer, not a king; and here he was expected to hold a king's state, and live in a king's publicity, but without the formal etiquette that hedge a king from intruders, and make his position tolerable. He was hemmed in by curious eyes, mobbed in the streets, stared at in his own private rooms, interviewed by the hour, shaken by the hand till his arm must often have been ready to drop off, waylaid at every turn with formal addresses. If he went to church the people crowded into the adjacent pews, and the preacher preached at him. If he got into a public conveyance, every one inside insisted on an introduction, and the people outside— say before the train started—would pull down the windows and comment freely on his nose and eyes and personal appearance generally, some even touching him as if to see if he were real. He was safe from intrusion nowhere —no, not when he was washing and his wife in bed. Such attentions must have been exhausting to a degree that can scarcely be imagined. But there was more than mere physical weariness in his growing distaste for the United States. Perfectly outspoken at all times, and eager for the strife of tongues in any cause which he had at heart, it horrified him to find that he was expected not to express himself freely on such subjects as International Copyright, and that even in private, or semi-private intercourse, slavery was a topic to be avoided. Then I fear, too, that as he left cultured Boston behind, he was brought into close and habitual contact with natives whom` he did not appreciate. Rightly or wrongly, he took a strong dislike for Brother Jonathan as Brother Jonathan existed, in the rough, five and forty years ago. He was angered by that young gentleman's brag, offended by the rough familiarity of his manners, indignant at his determination by all means to acquire dollars, incensed by his utter want of care for literature and art, sickened by his tobacco-chewing and expectorations. So when Dickens gets to "Niagara Falls, upon the *English* side," he puts ten dashes under the word English; and, meeting two English officers, contrasts them in thought with the men whom he has just left, and seems, by note of exclamation and italics, to call upon the world to witness, "what *gentlemen*, what noblemen of nature they seemed!"

And Brother Jonathan, how did *he* regard his young guest? Well, Jonathan, great as he was, and greater as he was destined to be, did not possess the gift of prophecy, and could not of course foresee the scathing satire of "American Notes" and "Martin Chuzzlewit." But still, amid all his enthusiasm, I think there must have been a feeling of uneasiness and disappointment. Part, as there is no doubt, of the fervour with which he greeted Dickens, was due to his regarding Dickens as the representative of democratic feeling in aristocratic England, as the advocate of the poor and down-trodden against the wealthy and the strong; "and"—thus argued Jonathan—"because

we are a democracy, therefore Dickens will admire and
love us, and see how immeasurably superior we are to the
retrograde Britishers of his native land." But unfortunately Dickens showed no signs of being impressed in
that particular way. On the contrary, as we have seen,
such comparison as he made in his own mind was infinitely to the disadvantage of the United States. " We
must be cracked up," says Hannibal Chollop, in " Martin
Chuzzlewit," speaking of his fellow countrymen. And
Dickens, even while fêted and honoured, would not
" crack up " the Americans. He lectured them almost
with truculence on their sins in the matter of copyright;
he could scarcely be restrained from testifying against
slavery; he was not the man to say he liked manners
and customs which he loathed. Jonathan must have
been very doubtfully satisfied with his guest.

It is no part of my purpose to follow Dickens linger-
ingly, and step by step, from the day when he landed at
Halifax, to the 7th of June, when he re-embarked at New
York for England. From Boston he went to New York,
where the great dinner was given with Washington Irving
in the chair, and thence to Philadelphia and Washington,
—which was still the empty "city of magnificent dis-
tances," that Mr. Goldwin Smith declares it has now
ceased to be ;—and thence again westward, and by Niagara
and Canada back to New York. And if any persons
want to know what he thought about these and other
places, and the railway travelling, and the coach travelling, and the steamboat travelling, and the prisons and
other public institutions—aye, and many other things
besides, they cannot do better than read the " Ameri- .

can Notes for general circulation," which he wrote and published within the year after his return. Nor need such persons be deterred by the fact that Macaulay thought meanly of the book; for Macaulay, with all his great gifts, did not, as he himself knew full well, excel in purely literary criticism. So when he pronounces, that "what is meant to be easy and sprightly is vulgar and flippant," and "what is meant to be fine is a great deal too fine for me, as the description of the Falls of Niagara," one can venture to differ without too great a pang. The book, though not assuredly one of Dickens' best, contains admirable passages which none but he could have written, and the description of Niagara is noticeably fine, the sublimity of the subject being remembered, as a piece of impassioned prose. Whether satire so bitter and unfriendly as that in which he indulged, both here and in "Martin Chuzzlewit," was justifiable from what may be called an international point of view, is another question. Publicists do not always remember that a cut which would smart for a moment, and then be forgotten, if aimed at a countryman, rankles and festers if administered to a foreigner. And if this be true as regards the English publicist's comment on the foreigner who does not understand our language, it is, of course, true with tenfold force as regards the foreigner whose language is our own. *He* understands only too well the jibe and the sneer, and the tone of superiority, more offensive perhaps than either. Looked at in this way, it can, I think, but be accounted a misfortune that the most popular of English writers penned two books containing so much calculated to wound American feeling, as the "Notes" and "Martin Chuzzlewit." Nor are signs entirely wanting that, as the years went by, the mind of Dickens himself was haunted by some such suspicion. A quarter of a century later, he visited the United States a second time; and speaking at a public dinner given in his honour by the journalists of New York, he took occasion to comment on the enormous strides which the country had made in the interval, and then said, "Nor am I, believe me, so arrogant as to suppose that in five and twenty years there have been no changes in me, and that I had nothing to learn, and no extreme impressions to correct when I was here first.' And he added that, in all future editions of the two books just named, he would cause to be recorded, that, "wherever he had been, in the smallest place equally with the largest, he had been received with unsurpassable politeness, delicacy, sweet temper, hospitality, consideration, and with unsurpassable respect for the privacy daily enforced upon him by the nature of his avocation there" (as a public reader), "and the state of his health."

And now, with three observations, I will conclude what I have to say about the visit to America in 1842. The first is that the "Notes" are entirely void of all vulgarity of reference to the private life of the notable Americans whom Dickens had met. He seems to have known, more or less intimately, the chief writers of the time—Washington Irving, Channing, Dana, Bryant, Longfellow, Bancroft; but his intercourse with them he held sacred, and he made no literary capital out of it. Secondly, it is pleasant to note that there was, so far, no great "incompatibility of temper" between him and his wife.

6

He speaks of her enthusiastically, in his correspondence, as a "most admirable traveller," and expatiates on the good temper and equanimity with which she had borne the fatigues and jars of a most trying journey. And the third point to which I will call attention is the thoroughly characteristic form of rest to which he had recourse in the midst of all his toil and travel. Most men would have sought relaxation in being quiet. He found it in vigorously getting up private theatricals with the officers of the Coldstream Guards, at Montreal. Besides acting in all the three pieces played, he also accepted the part of stage manager; and "I am not," he says, "placarded as stage manager for nothing. Everybody was told that they would have to submit to the most iron despotism, and didn't I come Macready over them? Oh no, by no means; certainly not. The pains I have taken with them, and the perspiration I have expended, during the last ten days, exceed in amount anything you can imagine." What bright vitality, and what a singular charm of exuberant animal spirits!

And who was glad one evening—which would be about the last evening in June, or the first of July—when a hackney coach rattled up to the door of the house in Devonshire Terrace, and four little folk, two girls and two boys, were hurried down, and kissed through the bars of the gate, because their father was too eager to wait till it was opened? Who were glad but the little folk aforementioned—I say nothing of the joy of father and mother; for children as they were, a sense of sorrowful loss had been theirs while their parents were away, and greater strictness seems to have reigned in the good Macready's household than in their own joyous home. It is Miss Dickens herself who tells us this, and in whose memory has lingered that pretty scene of the kiss through the bars in the summer gloaming. And she has much to tell us too of her father's tenderness and care,—of his sympathy with the children's terrors, so that, for instance, he would sit beside the cot of one of the little girls who had been startled, and hold her hand in his till she fell asleep; of his having them on his knees, and singing to them the merriest of comic songs ; of his interest in all their small concerns; of the many pet names with which he invested them.[1] Then, as they grew older, there were Twelfth Night parties and magic lanterns. "Never such magic lanterns as those shown by him," she says. "Never such conjuring as his." There was dancing, too, and the little ones taught him his steps, which he practised with much assiduity, once even jumping out of bed in terror, lest he had forgotten the polka, and indulging in a solitary midnight rehearsal. Then, as the children grew older still, there were private theatricals. "He never," she says again, "was too busy to interest himself in his children's occupations, lessons, amusements, and general welfare." Clearly not one of those brilliant men, a numerous race, who when away from their homes, in general society, sparkle and scintillate, flash out their wit, and irradiate all with their humour, but who, when at home, are dull as rusted steel. Among the many tributes to his greatness, that of his own child has a place at once touching and beautiful.

[1] Miss Dickens evidently bears proudly still her pet name of " Mamie," and signs it to her book.

CHAPTER VII.

WITH the return from America began the old life of hard work and hard play. There was much industrious writing of "American Notes," at Broadstairs and elsewhere; and there were many dinners of welcome home, and strolls, doubtless, with Forster and Maclise, and other intimates, to old haunts, as Jack Straw's Castle on Hampstead Heath, and similar houses of public entertainment. And then in the autumn there was "such a trip . . . into Cornwall," with Forster, and the painters Stanfield and Maclise for travelling companions. How they enjoyed themselves to be sure, and with what bubbling, bursting merriment. "I never laughed in my life as I did on this journey," writes Dickens, ". . . I was choking and gasping . . . all the way. And Stanfield got into such apoplectic entanglements that we were often obliged to beat him on the back with portmanteaus before we could recover him." Immediately on their return, refreshed and invigorated by this wholesome hilarity and enjoyment, he threw himself into the composition of his next book, and the first number of "Martin Chuzzlewit" appeared in January, 1843.

" Martin Chuzzlewit " is unquestionably one of
Dickens' great works. He himself held it to be "in a
hundred points " and "immeasurably " superior to anything he had before written, and that verdict may, I
think, be accepted freely. The plot, as plot is usually
understood, can scarcely indeed be commended. But
then plot was never his strong point. Later in life, and
acting, as I have always surmised, under the influence of
his friend, Mr. Wilkie Collins, he endeavoured to construct ingenious stories that turned on mysterious dis-
appearances, and the substitution of one person for
another, and murders real or suspected. All this was,
to my mind, a mistake. Dickens had no real gift for the
manufacture of these ingenious pieces of mechanism. He
did not even many times succeed in disposing the events
and marshalling the characters in his narratives so as to
work, by seemingly unforced and natural means, to a final
situation and climax. Too often, in order to hold his
story together and make it move forward at all, he was
compelled to make his personages pursue a line of conduct preposterous and improbable, and even antagonistic
to their nature. Take this very book. Old Martin
Chuzzlewit is a man who has been accustomed, all through
a long life, to have his own way, and to take it with a
high hand. Yet he so far sets aside, during a course of
months, every habit of his life, as to simulate the
weakest subservience to Pecksniff—and that not for the
purpose of unmasking Pecksniff, who wanted no unmasking, but only in order to disappoint him. Is it
believable that old Martin should have thought Pecksniff
worth so much trouble, personal inconvenience, and

humiliation? Or take again Mr. Boffin in " Our Mutual
Friend." Mr. Boffin is a simple, guileless, open-hearted,
open-handed old man. Yet, in order to prove to Miss
Bella Wilfer that it is not well to be mercenary, he, again,
goes through a long course of dissimulation, and does
some admirable comic business in the character of a
miser. I say it boldly, I do not believe Mr. Boffin possessed that amount of histrionic talent. Plots requiring
to be worked out by such means are ill-constructed plots ;
or, to put it in another way, a man who had any gift for
the construction of plots would never have had recourse
to such means. Nor would he, I think, have adopted,
as Dickens did habitually and for all his stories, a mode
of publication so destructive of unity of effect, as the
publication in monthly or weekly parts. How could the
reader see as a whole that which was presented to him at
intervals of time more or less distant? How, and this
is of infinitely greater importance, how could the writer
produce it as a whole? For Dickens, it must be remembered, never finished a book before the commencement of
publication. At first he scarcely did more than complete
each monthly instalment as required ; and though afterwards he was generally some little way in advance, yet
always he wrote by parts, having the interest of each
separate part in his mind, as well as the general interest
of the whole novel. Thus, however desirable in the
development of the story, he dared not risk a comparatively tame and uneventful number. Moreover, any
portion once issued was unalterable and irrevocable. If,
as sometimes happened, any modification seemed desirable as the book progressed, there was no possibility

of changing anything in the chapters already in the hands of the public, and so making them harmonize better with the new.

But of course, with all this, the question still remains how far Dickens' comparative failure as a constructor of plots really detracts from his fame and standing as a novelist. To my mind, I confess, not very much. Plot I regard as the least essential element in the novelist's art. A novel can take the very highest rank without it. There is not any plot to speak of in Lesage's " Gil Blas," and just as little in Thackeray's " Vanity Fair," and only a very bad one in Goldsmith's " Vicar of Wakefield." Coleridge admired the plot of " Tom Jones," but though one naturally hesitates to differ from a critic of such superb mastery and· power, I confess I have never been struck by that plot, any more than by the plots, such as they are, in " Joseph Andrews," or in Smollett's works. Nor, if I can judge of other people's memories by my own, is it by the mechanism of the story, or by the intrigue, however admirably woven and unravelled, that one remembers a work of fiction. These may exercise an intense passing interest of curiosity, especially during a first perusal. But afterwards they fade from the mind, while the characters, if highly vitalized and strong, will stand out in our thoughts, fresh and full coloured, for an indefinite time. Scott's " Guy Mannering " is a well-constructed story. The plot is deftly laid, the events are prepared for with a cunning hand ; the coincidences are so arranged as to be made to look as probable as may be. Yet we remember and love the book, not for such excellences as these, but for Dandie

Dinmont, the Border farmer, and Pleydell, the Edinburgh advocate, and Meg Merrilies, the gipsy. The book's life is in its flesh and blood, not in its plot. And the same is true of Dickens' novels. He crowds them so full of human creatures, each with its own individuality and character, that we have no care for more than just as much story as may serve to show them struggling, joying, sorrowing, loving. If the incidents will do this for us we are satisfied. It is not necessary that those incidents should be made to go through cunning evolutions to a definite end. Each is admirable in itself, and admirably adapted to its immediate purpose. That should more than suffice.

And Dickens sometimes succeeds in reaching a higher unity than that of mere plot. He takes one central idea, and makes of it the soul of his novel, animating and vivifying every part. That central idea in "Martin Chuzzlewit" is the influence of selfishness. The Chuzzlewits are a selfish race. Old Martin is selfish ; and so, with many good qualities and possibilities of better things, is his grandson, young Martin. The other branch of the family, Anthony Chuzzlewit and his son Jonas, are much worse. The latter especially is a horrible creature. Brought up to think of nothing except his own interests and the main chance, he is only saved by an accident from the crime of parricide, and afterwards commits a murder and poisons himself. As his career is one of terrible descent, so young Martin's is one of gradual regeneration from his besetting weakness. He falls in love with his cousin Mary—the only unselfish member of the family, by the bye—and quarrels about this love affair with his grandfather, and so passes into the hard school of adversity. There he learns much. Specially valuable is the teaching which he gets as a settler in the swampy backwoods of the United States in company with Mark Tapley, jolliest and most helpful of men. On his return, he finds his grandfather seemingly under the influence of Pecksniff, the hypocrite, the English Tartuffe. But that, as I have already mentioned, is only a ruse. Old Martin is deceiving Pecksniff, who in due time receives the reward of his deeds, and all ends happily for those who deserve happiness. Such is something like a bare outline of the story, with the beauty eliminated. For what makes its interest, we must go further, to the household of Pecksniff with his two daughters, Charity and Mercy, and Tom Pinch, whose beautiful, unselfish character stands so in contrast to that of the grasping self-seekers by whom he is surrounded; we must study young Martin himself, whose character is admirably drawn, and without Dickens' usual tendency to caricature; we must laugh in sympathy with Mark Tapley; we must follow them both through the American scenes, which, intensely amusing as they are, must have bitterly envenomed the wounds inflicted on the national vanity by "American Notes," and, according to Dickens' own expression, "sent them all stark staring raving mad across the water;" we must frequent the boarding establishment for single gentlemen kept by lean Mrs. Todgers, and sit with Sarah Gamp and Betsy Prig as they hideously discuss their avocations, or quarrel over the shadowy Mrs. Harris; we must follow Jonas Chuzzlewit on his errand of

murder, and note how even his felon nature is appalled
by the blackness and horror of his guilt, and how the
ghastly terror of it haunts and cows him. A great book,
I say again, a very great book.

Yet not at the time a successful book. Why Fortune,
the fickle jade, should have taken it into her freakish
head to frown, or half frown, on Dickens at this particular juncture, who shall tell? He was wooing her with
his very best work, and she turned from him. The sale
of "Pickwick" and "Nicholas Nickleby" had been from
forty to fifty thousand copies of each part; the sale
of *Master Humphrey's Clock* had risen still higher; the
sale of even the most popular parts of "Martin Chuzzlewit" fell to twenty-three thousand. This was, as may be
supposed, a grievous disappointment. Dickens' personal
expenditure had not perhaps been lavish in view of
what he thought he could calculate on earning; but it
had been freely based on that calculation. Demands,
too, were being made upon his purse by relations,—
probably by his father, and certainly by his brother
Frederic, which were frequent, embarrassing, and made
in a way which one may call worse than indelicate. Any
permanent loss of popularity would have meant serious
money entanglements. With his father's career in full
view, such a prospect must have been anything but
pleasant. He cast about what he should do, and
determined to leave England for a space, live more
economically on the Continent, and gather materials in
Italy or Switzerland for a new travel book. But before
carrying out this project, he would woo fortune once
again, and in a different form. During the months of

October and November, 1843, in the intervals of
" Chuzzlewit," he wrote a short story that has taken its
place, by almost universal consent, among his masterpieces, nay, among the masterpieces of English literature : " The Christmas Carol."

All Dickens' great gifts seem reflected, . sharp and
distinct, in this little book, as in a convex mirror. His
humour, his best pathos, which is not that of grandilo-
quence, but of simplicity, his bright poetic fancy, his
kindliness, all here find a place. It is great painting in
miniature, genius in its quintessence, a gem of perfect water.
We may apply to it any simile that implies excellence
in the smallest compass. None but a fine imagination
would have conceived the supernatural agency that works
old Scrooge's moral regeneration—the ghosts of Christmas
past, present, and to come, that each in turn speaks to
the wizened heart of the old miser, so that, almost
unwittingly, he is softened by the tender memories
of childhood, warmed by sympathy for those who
struggle and suffer, and appalled by the prospect of his
own ultimate desolation and black solitude. Then the
episodes : the scenes to which these ghostly visitants
convey Scrooge ; the story of his earlier years as shown
in vision ; the household of the Cratchits, and poor
little crippled Tiny Tim ; the party given by Scrooge's
nephew ; nay, before all these, the terrible interview with
Marley's Ghost. All are admirably executed. Sacrilege
would it be to suggest the alteration of a word. First of
the Christmas books in the order of time, it is also the
best of its own kind ; it is in its own order perfect.

Nor did the public of Christmas, 1843, fail to appreciate

that something of very excellent quality had been brought
forth for their benefit. " The first edition of six thousand
copies," says Forster, " was sold " on the day of publication, and about as many more would seem to have been
disposed of before the end of February, 1844. But, alas,
Dickens had set his heart on a profit of £1,000, whereas
in February he did not see his way to much more than
£460,[1] and his unpaid bills for the previous year he
described as " terrific." So something, as I have said,
had to be done. A change of front became imperative.
Messrs. Bradbury and Evans advanced him £2,800 " for
a fourth share in whatever he might write during the
ensuing eight years,"—he purchased at the Pantechnicon
" a good old shabby devil of a coach," also described as
" an English travelling carriage of considerable proportions " ; engaged a courier who turned out to be the
courier of couriers, a very conjurer among couriers ; let
his house in Devonshire Terrace ; and so started off for
Italy, as I calculate the dates, on the 1st of July, 1844.

[1] The profit at the end of 1844 was £726.

CHAPTER VIII.

A H, those eventful, picturesque, uncomfortable old travelling days, when railways were unborn, or in their infancy; those interminable old dusty drives, in diligence or private carriage, along miles and miles of roads running straight to the low horizon, through a line of tall poplars, across the plains of France ! What an old-world memory it seems, and yet, as the years go, not so very long since after all. The party that rumbled from Boulogne to Marseilles in the old " devil of a coach " aforesaid, " and another conveyance for luggage," and I know not what other conveyances besides, consisted of Dickens himself ; Mrs. Dickens ; her sister, Miss Georgina Hogarth, who had come to live with them on their return from America ; five children, for another boy had been born some six months before ; Roche, the prince of couriers ; "Anne," apparently the same maid who had accompanied them across the Atlantic ; and other dependents : a somewhat formidable troupe and cavalcade. Of their mode of travel, and what they saw on the way, or perhaps, more accurately, of what Dickens saw, with those specially keen eyes of his, at

Lyons, Avignon, Marseilles, and other places—one may read the master's own account in the "Pictures from Italy." Marseilles was reached on the 14th of July, and thence a steamer took them, coasting the fairy Mediterranean shores, to Genoa, their ultimate destination, where they landed on the 16th.

The Italy of 1844 was like, and yet unlike the Italy of to-day. It was the old disunited Italy of several small kingdoms and principalities, the Italy over which lowered the shadow of despotic Austria, and of the Pope's temporal power, not the Italy which the genius of Cavour has welded into a nation. It was a land whose interest came altogether from the past, and that lay as it were in the beauty of time's sunset. How unlike the United States ! The contrast has always, I confess, seemed to me a piquant one. It has often struck me with a feeling of quaintness that the two countries which Dickens specially visited and described, were, the one this lovely land of age and hoar antiquity, and the other that young giant land of the West, which is still in the garish strong light of morning, and whose great day is in the future. Nor, I think, before he had seen both, would Dickens himself have been able to tell on which side his sympathies would lie. Thoroughly popular in his convictions, thoroughly satisfied that to-day was in all respects better than yesterday, it is clear that he expected to find more pleasure in the brand new Republic than his actual experience warranted. The roughness of the strong, uncultured young life grated upon him. It jarred upon his sensibilities. But of Italy he wrote with very different feeling. What though the places were dirty, the people shiftless, idle, unpunctual, unbusinesslike, and the fleas as the sand which is upon the sea-shore for multitude? It mattered not while life was so picturesque and varied, and manners were so full of amenity. Your inn might be, and probably was, ill-appointed, untidy, the floors of brick, the doors agape, the windows banging—a contrast in every way to the palatial hotel in New York or Washington. But then how cheerful and amusing were mine host and hostess, and how smilingly determined all concerned to make things pleasant. So the artist in Dickens turned from the new to the old, and Italy, as she is wont, cast upon him her spell.

First impressions, however, were not altogether satisfactory. Dickens owns to a pang when he was "set down" at Albaro, a suburb of Genoa, "in a rank, dull, weedy courtyard, attached to a kind of pink jail, and told he lived there." But he immediately adds: "I little thought that day that I should ever come to have an attachment for the very stones in the streets of Genoa, and to look back upon the city with affection, as connected with many hours of happiness and quiet." In sooth, he enjoyed the place thoroughly. "Martin Chuzzlewit" had left his hands. He was fairly entitled for a few weeks to the luxury of idleness, and he threw himself into doing nothing, as he was accustomed to throw himself into his work, with all energy. And there was much to do, much especially to see. So Dickens bathed and walked; and strolled about the city hither and thither, and about the suburbs and about the surrounding country; and visited public buildings and private palaces; and noted the ways of the inhabitants; and saw Genoese life in its varied

forms ; and wrote light glancing letters about it all to
friends at home ; and learnt Italian ; and, in the end of
September, left his "pink jail," which had been taken for
him at a disproportionate rent, and moved into the Palazzo
Peschiere, in Genoa itself : a wonderful palace, with an
entrance-hall fifty feet high, and larger than "the dining-
room of the Academy," and bedrooms " in size and shape
like those at Windsor Castle, but greatly higher," and
a view from the windows over gardens where the many
fountains sparkled, and the gold fish glinted, and into
Genoa itself, with its " many churches, monasteries, and
convents pointing to the sunny sky," and into the harbour,
and over the sapphire sea, and up again to the encircling
hills—a view, as Dickens declared, that "no custom
could impair, and no description enhance."

But with the beginning of October came again the
time for work ; and beautiful beyond all beauty as were
his surroundings, the child of London turned to the home
of his heart, and pined for the London streets. For some
little space he seemed to be thinking in vain, and cudgel-
ling his brains for naught, when suddenly the chimes of
Genoa's many churches, that seemed to have been clash-
ing and clanging nothing but distraction and madness,
rang harmony into his mind. The subject and title of his
new Christmas book were found. He threw himself into
the composition of " The Chimes."

Earnest at all times in what he wrote, living ever in
intense and passionate sympathy with the world of his
imagination, he seems specially to have put his whole
heart into this book. "All my affections and passions
got twined and knotted up in it, and I became as haggard

as a murderer long before I wrote 'the end,'"—so he
told Lady Blessington on the 20th of November; and to
Forster he expressed the yearning that was in him to
" leave" his " hand upon the time, lastingly upon the time,
with one tender touch for the mass of toiling people that
nothing could obliterate." This was the keynote of
"The Chimes." He intended in it to strike a great and
memorable blow on behalf of the poor and down-trodden.
His purpose, so far as I can make it out, was to show
how much excuse there is for their shortcomings, and
how in their errors, nay even in their crimes, there linger
traces of goodness and kindly feeling. On this I shall
have something to say when discussing " Hard Times,"
which is somewhat akin to " The Chimes " in scope and
purpose. Meanwhile it cannot honestly be affirmed that
the story justifies the passion that Dickens threw into
its composition. The supernatural machinery is weak as
compared with that of the "Carol." Little Trotty Veck,
dreaming to the sound of the bells in the old church
tower, is a bad substitute for Scrooge on his midnight
rambles. Nor are his dreams at all equal, for humour
or pathos, to Scrooge's visions and experiences. And
the moral itself is not clearly brought out. I confess to
being a little doubtful as to what it exactly is, and how it
follows from the premises furnished. I wish, too, that it
had been carried home to some one with more power than
little Trotty to give it effect. What was the good of
convincing that kindly old soul that the people of his
own class had warm hearts? He knew it very well.
Take from the book the fine imaginative description of
the goblin music that leaps into life with the ringing of

7

the bells, and there remain the most excellent intentions
—and not much more.

Such, however, was very far from being Dickens' view.
He had "undergone," he said, "as much sorrow and
agitation" in the writing "as if the thing were real," and
on the 3rd of November, when the last page was written,
had indulged "in what women call a good cry;" and, as
usually happens, the child that had cost much sorrow was
a child of special love.[1] So, when all was over, nothing
would do but he must come to London to read his book
to the choice literary spirits whom he specially loved.
Accordingly he started from Genoa on the 6th of
November, travelled by Parma, Modena, Bologna, Fer-
rara, Venice—where, such was the enchantment of the
place, that he felt it "cruel not to have brought Kate and
Georgy, positively cruel and base";—and thence again by
Verona, Mantua, Milan, the Simplon Pass, Strasbourg, Paris,
and Calais, to Dover, and wintry England. Sharp work, considering all he had seen by the way, and how effectually he
had seen it, for he was in London on the evening of the
30th of November, and, on the 2nd of December, reading
his little book to the choice spirits aforesaid, all assembled
for the purpose at Forster's house. There they are: they
live for us still in Maclise's drawing, though Time has
plied his scythe among them so effectually, during the
forty-two years since flown, that each has passed into the
silent land. There they sit: Carlyle, not the shaggy
Scotch terrier with the melancholy eyes that we were
wont to see in his later days, but close shaven and alert;
and swift-witted Douglas Jerrold; and Laman Blanchard,

[1] He read "The Chimes" at his first reading as a paid reader.

whose name goes darkling in the literature of the last
generation ; and Forster himself, journalist and author of
many books ; and the painters Dyce, Maclise, and Stanfield ; and Byron's friend and school companion, the
clergyman Harness, who, like Dyce, pays to the story the
tribute of his tears.

Dickens can have been in London but the fewest of
few days, for on the 13th of December he was leaving
Paris for Genoa, and that after going to the theatre more
than once. From Genoa he started again, on the 20th
of January, 1845, with Mrs. Dickens, to see the Carnival
at Rome. Thence he went to Naples, returning to
Rome for the Holy Week ; and thence again by Florence
to Genoa. He finally left Italy in the beginning of June,
and was back with his family in Devonshire Terrace at
the end of that month.

To what use of a literary kind should he turn his
Italian observations and experiences ? In what form
should he publish the notes made by the way ? Events
soon answered that question. The year 1845 stands in
the history of Queen Victoria's reign as a time of intense
political excitement. The Corn Law agitation raged
somewhat furiously. Dickens felt strongly impelled to
throw himself into the strife. Why should he not influence his fellow-men, and "battle for the true, the just,"
as the able editor of a daily newspaper ? Accordingly,
after all the negotiations which enterprises of this kind
necessitate, he made the due arrangements for starting a
new paper, *The Daily News.* It was to be edited by
himself, to "be kept free," the prospectus said, "from
personal influence or party bias," and to be " devoted to

the advocacy of all rational and honest means by which
wrong may be redressed, just rights maintained, and the
happiness and welfare of society promoted." His salary,
so I have seen it stated, was to be £2,000 a year; and
the first number came out on the morning of the 21st
of January, 1846. He held the post of editor three
weeks.

The world may, I think, on the whole, be congratulated
that he did not hold it longer. Able editors are more
easily found than such writers as Dickens. There were
higher claims upon his time. But to return to the
Italian Notes : it was in the columns of *The
Daily News* that they first saw the light. They were
among the baby attractions and charms, if I may so
speak, of the nascent paper, which is now, as I need not
remind my readers, enjoying a hale and vigorous manhood. And admirable sketches they are. Much, very
much has been written about Italy. The subject has
been done to death by every variety of pen, and in every
civilized tongue. But amid all this writing, Dickens'
" Pictures from Italy " still holds a high and distinctive
position. That the descriptions, whether of places and
works of art, or of life's pageantry, and what may be called
the social picturesque, should be graphic, vivid, animated,
was almost a matter of course. But *à priori*, I think one
might have feared lest he should " chaff " the place and
its inhabitants overmuch, and yield to the temptation of
making merriment over matters which hoar age and old
associations had hallowed. We can all imagine the kind
of observation that would occur to Sam Weller in strolling
through St. Mark's at Venice, or the Vatican; and, guessing

beforehand, guessing before the "Pictures" were produced, one might, I repeat, have been afraid lest Dickens should go through Italy as a kind of educated Sam Weller. Such prophecies would have been falsified by the event. The book as a whole is very free from banter or *persiflage*. Once and again the comic side of some situation strikes him, of course. Thus, after the ceremony of the Pope washing the feet of thirteen poor men, in memory of our Lord washing the feet of the Apostles, Dickens says : " The whole thirteen sat down to dinner ; grace said by the Pope ; Peter in the chair." But these humorous touches are rare, and not in bad taste ; while for the historic and artistic grandeurs of Italy he shows an enthusiasm which is *individual* and discriminating. We feel, in what he says about painting, that we are getting the fresh impressions of a man not specially trained in the study of the old masters, but who yet succeeds, by sheer intuitive sympathy ; in appreciating much of their greatness. His criticism of the paintings at Venice, for instance, is very decidedly superior to that of Macaulay. In brief the " Pictures," to give to the book the name which Dickens gave it, are painted with a brush at once kindly and brilliant.

CHAPTER IX

THE publication of the "Pictures," though I have dealt with it as a sort of complement to Dickens' sojourn in Italy, carries us to the year 1846. But before going on with the history of that year, there are one or two points to be taken up in the history of 1845. The first is the performance, on the 21st of September, of Ben Jonson's play of "Every Man in his Humour," by a select company of amateur actors, among whom Dickens held chief place. "He was the life and soul of the entire affair," says Forster. "I never seem till then to have known his business capabilities. He took everything on himself, and did the whole of it without an effort. He was stage director, very often stage carpenter, scene arranger, property man, prompter, and band-master. Without offending any one, he kept every one in order. For all he had useful suggestions. . . . He adjusted scenes, assisted carpenters, invented costumes, devised playbills, wrote out calls, and enforced, as well as exhibited in his own proper person, everything of which he urged the necessity on others." Dickens had once thought of the stage as a profession, and was, according to all accounts, an amateur actor of very unusual power.

But of course he only acted for his amusement, and I don't know that I should have dwelt upon this perform-ance, which was followed by others of a similar kind, if it did not, in Forster's description, afford such a signal instance of his efficiency as a practical man. The second event to be mentioned as happening in 1845, is the pub-lication of another very pretty Christmas story, "The Cricket on the Hearth."

Though Dickens had ceased to edit *The Daily News* on the 9th of February, 1846, he contributed to the paper for some few weeks longer. But by the month of May his connection with it had entirely ceased; and on the 31st of that month, he started, by Belgium and the Rhine, for Lausanne in Switzerland, where he had deter-mined to spend some time, and commence his next great book, and write his next Christmas story.

A beautiful place is Lausanne, as many of my readers will know; and a beautiful house the house called Rosemont, situated on a hill that rises from the Lake of Geneva, with the lake's blue waters stretching below, and across, on the other side, a magnificent panorama of snowy mountains, the Simplon, St. Gothard, Mont Blanc, towering to the sky. This delightful place Dickens took at a rent of some £10 a month. Then he re-arranged all the furniture, as was his energetic wont. Then he spent a fortnight or so in looking about him, and writing a good deal for Lord John Russell on Ragged Schools, and for Miss Coutts about her various charities; and finally, on the 28th of June, as he announced to Forster in capital letters, BEGAN DOMBEY.

But as the Swiss pine with home-sickness when away

from their own dear land, so did this Londoner, amid all
the glories of the Alps, pine for the London streets. It
seemed almost as if they were essential to the exercise of
his genius. The same strange mental phenomenon which
he had observed in himself at Genoa was reproduced here.
Everything else in his surroundings smiled most con-
genially. The place was fair beyond speech. The
shifting, changing beauty of the mountains entranced
him. . The walks offered an endless variety of enjoyment.
He liked the people. He liked the English colony. He
had made several dear friends among them and among
the natives. He was interested in the politics of the
country, which happened, just then, to be in a state of
peculiar excitement and revolution. Everything was
charming;—"but," he writes, "the toil and labour of
writing, day after day, without that magic-lantern (of the
London streets) is IMMENSE!" It literally knocked him
up. He had "bad nights," was "sick and giddy," de-
sponding over his book, more than half inclined to
abandon the Christmas story altogether for that year.
However, a short trip to Geneva, and the dissipation of
a stroll or so in its thoroughfares, to remind him, as it
were, of what streets were like, and a week of "idleness"
"rusting and devouring," "complete and unbroken,"
set him comparatively on his legs again, and before he
left Lausanne for Paris on the 16th of November, he had
finished three parts of " Dombey," and the " Battle of
Life."

Of the latter I don't know that I need say anything.
It is decidedly the weakest of his Christmas books. But
" Dombey " is very different work, and the first five

numbers especially, which carry the story to the death of little Paul, contain passages of humour and pathos, and of humour and pathos mingled together and shot in warp and woof, like some daintiest silken fabric, that are scarcely to be matched in the language. As I go in my mind through the motherless child's short history—his birth, his christening, the engagement of the wet-nurse, the time when he is consigned to the loveless care of Mrs. Pipchin, his education in Dr. Blimber's Academy under the classic Cornelia, and his death—as I follow it all in thought, now smiling at each well-remembered touch of humour, and now saddened and solemnized as the shadow of death deepens over the frail little life, I confess to something more than critical admiration for the writer as an artist. I feel towards him as towards one who has touched my heart. Of course it is the misfortune of the book, regarding it as a whole, that the chapters relating to Paul, which are only an episode, should be of such absorbing interest, and come so early. Dickens really wrote them too well. They dwarf the rest of the story. We find a difficulty in resuming the thread of it with the same zest when the child is gone. But though the remainder of the book inevitably suffers in this way, it ought not to suffer unduly. Even apart from little Paul the novel is a fine one. Pride is its subject, as selfishness is that of " Martin Chuzzlewit." Mr. Dombey, the city merchant, has as much of the arrogance of caste and position as any blue-blooded hidalgo. He is as proud of his name as if he had inherited it from a race of princes. That he neglects and slights his daughter, and loves his son, is mainly because the latter will add a sort

of completeness to the firm, and make it truly Dombey
and Son, while the girl, for all commercial purposes, can
be nothing but a cipher. And through his pride he is
struck to the heart, and ruined. Mr. Carker, his confidential agent and manager, trades upon it for all vile
ends, first to feather his own nest, and then to launch his
patron into large and unsound business ventures. The
second wife, whom he marries, certainly with no affection
on either side, but purely because of her birth and connections, and because her great beauty will add to his
social prestige—she, with ungovernable pride equal to his
own, revolts against his authority, and, in order to humiliate
him the more, pretends to elope with Carker, whom in
turn she scorns and crushes. Broken thus in fortune and
honour, Mr. Dombey yet falls not ignobly. His creditors
he satisfies in full, reserving to himself nothing ; and with
a softened heart turns to the daughter he had slighted,
and in her love finds comfort. Such is the main purport
of the story, and round it, in graceful arabesques, are
embroidered, after Dickens' manner, a whole world of
subsidiary incidents thronged with all sorts of characters.
What might not one say about Dr. Blimber's genteel
academy at Brighton ; and the Toodles family, so humble in station and intellect and so large of heart ; and the
contrast between Carker the manager and his brother,
who for some early dishonest act, long since repented of,
remains always Carker the junior ; and about Captain
Cuttle, and that poor, muddled nautical philosopher,
Captain Bunsby, and the Game Chicken, and Mrs.
Pipchin, and Miss Tox ; and Cousin Feenix with wilful
legs so little under control, and yet to the core of

him a gentleman; and the apoplectic Major Bagstock,
the Joey B. who claimed to be "rough and tough and
devilish sly;" and Susan Nipper, as swift of tongue as a
rapier, and as sharp? Reader, don't you know all these
people? For myself, I have jostled against them constantly any time the last twenty years. They are as
much part of my life as the people I meet every day.

But there is one person whom I have left out of my
ennumeration, not certainly because I don't know him,
for I know him very well, but because I want to speak
about him more particularly. That person is my old
friend, Mr. Toots; and the special point in his character
which induces me to linger is the slight touch of craziness
that sits so charmingly upon him. M. Taine, the French
critic, in his chapters on Dickens, repeats the old remark
that genius and madness are near akin.[1] He observes,
and observes truly, that Dickens describes so well because an imagination of singular intensity enables him to
see the object presented, and at the same time to impart
to it a kind of visionary life. "That imagination," says
M. Taine, "is akin to the imagination of the mono-
maniac." And, starting from this point, he proceeds to
show, here again quite truly, with what admirable sympathetic power and insight Dickens has described certain
cases of madness, as in Mr. Dick. But here, having said
some right things, M. Taine goes all wrong. According
to him, these portraits of persons who have lost their
wits, "however amusing they may seem at first sight,
are "horrible." They could only have been painted by
"an imagination such as that of Dickens, excessive, dis-

[1] "History of English Literature," vol. v.

ordered, and capable of hallucination." He seems to be not far from thinking that only our splenetic and melancholy race could have given birth to such literary monsters. To speak like this, as I conceive, shows a singular misconception of the instinct or set purpose that led Dickens to introduce these characters into his novels at all. It is perfectly true that he has done so several times. Barnaby Rudge, the hero of the book of the same name, is half-witted. Mr. Dick, in " David Copperfield," is decidedly crazy. Mr. Toots is at least simple. Little Miss Flite, in " Bleak House," haunting the Law Courts in expectation of a judgment on the Day of Judgment, is certainly not *compos mentis*. And one may concede to M. Taine that some element of sadness must always be present when we see a human creature imperfectly gifted with man's noblest attribute of reason. But, granting this to the full, is it possible to conceive of anything more kindly and gentle in the delineation of partial insanity than the portraits which the French critic finds horrible? Barnaby Rudge's lunatic symptoms are compatible with the keenest enjoyment of nature's sights and sounds, fresh air and free sunlight, and compatible with loyalty and high courage. Many men might profitably change their reason for his unreason. Mr. Dick's flightiness is allied to an intense devotion and gratitude to the woman who had rescued him from confinement in an asylum ; there lives a world of kindly sentiments in his poor bewildered brains. Of Mr. Toots, Susan Nipper says truly, " he may not be a Solomon, nor do I say he is, but this I do say, a less selfish human creature human nature never knew." And to this one may add that he is entirely high-minded, generous, and honourable. Miss Flite's crazes do not prevent her from being full of all womanly sympathies. Here I think lies the charm these characters had for Dickens. As he was fond of showing a soul of goodness in the ill-favoured and un-couth, so he liked to make men feel that even in a dis-ordered intellect all kindly virtues might find a home, and a happy one. M. Taine may call this "horrible" if he likes. - I think myself it would be possible to find a better adjective.

Dickens was at work on "Dombey and Son" during the latter part of the year 1846, and the whole of 1847, and the early part of 1848. We left him on the 16th of November, in the first of these years, starting from Lausanne for Paris, which he reached on the evening of the 20th. Here he took a house—a "prepos-terous" house, according to his own account, with only gleams of reason in it; and visited many theatres; and went very often to the Morgue, where lie the unowned dead; and had pleasant friendly intercourse with the notable French authors of the time, Alexandre Dumas the Great, most prolific of romance writers; and Scribe of the innumerable plays; and the poets Lamartine and Victor Hugo; and Chateaubriand, then in his sad and somewhat morose old age. And in Paris too, with the help of streets and crowded ways, he wrote the great number of Dombey, the number in which little Paul dies. Three months did Dickens spend in the French capital, the incomparable city, and then was back in London, at the old life of hard work; but with even a stronger

infusion than before of private theatricals—private
theatricals on a grandiose scale, that were applauded by
the Queen herself, and took him and his troupe starring
about during the next three or four years, hither and
thither, and here and there, in London and the provinces.
"Splendid strolling" Forster calls it; and a period of
unmixed jollity and enjoyment it seems to have been.
Of course Dickens was the life and soul of it all. Mrs.
Cowden Clarke, one of the few survivors, looking back
to that happy time, says enthusiastically, "Charles
Dickens, beaming in look, alert in manner, radiant with
good humour, genial-voiced, gay, the very soul of enjoyment, fun, good taste, and good spirits, admirable in
organizing details and suggesting novelty of entertainment, was of all beings the very man for a holiday season."[1]
The proceeds of the performances were devoted to various
objects, but chiefly to an impossible "Guild of Literature
and Art," which, in the sanguine confidence of its projec-
tors, and especially of Dickens, was to inaugurate a golden
age for the author and the artist. But of all this, and of
Dickens' speeches at the Leeds Mechanics' Institute, and
Glasgow Athenæum, in the December of 1847, I don't know
that I need say very much. The interest of a great writer's
life is, after all, mainly in what he writes; and when I
have said that "Dombey" proved to be a pecuniary success, the first six numbers realizing as much as £2,820,
I think I may fairly pass on to Dickens' next book, the
"Haunted Man."

This was his Christmas story for 1848; the last, and

[1] "Recollections of Writers," by Charles and Mary Cowden
Clarke.

not the worst of his Christmas stories. Both conception
and treatment are thoroughly characteristic. Mr. Redlaw,
a chemist, brooding over an ancient wrong, comes to the
conclusion that it would be better for himself, better for
all, if, in each of us, every memory of the past could be
cancelled. A ghostly visitant, born of his own resent-
ment and gloom, gives him the boon he seeks, and
enables him to go about the world freezing all recollection
in those he meets. And lo the boon turns out to be a
curse. His presence blights those on whom it falls. For
with the memory of past wrongs, goes the memory of past
benefits, of all the mutual kindlinesses of life, and each
unit of humanity becomes self-centred and selfish.
Two beings alone resist his influence—one, a creature
too selfishly nurtured for any of mankind's better recollections; and the other a woman so good as to resist the
spell, and even, finally, to exorcise it in Mr. Redlaw's
own breast.

"David Copperfield" was published between May,
1849, and the autumn of 1850, and marks, I think, the
culminating point in Dickens' career as a writer. So far
there had been, not perhaps from book to book, but on
the whole, decided progress, the gradual attainment of
greater ease, and of the power of obtaining results of equal
power by simpler means. Beyond this there was, if not
absolute declension, for he never wrote anything that
could properly be called careless and unworthy of himself,
yet at least no advance. Of the interest that attaches to
the book from the fact that so many portions are autobiographical, I have already spoken; nor need I go over
the ground again. But quite apart from such adventitious

attractions, the novel is an admirable one. All the scenes
of little David's childhood in the Norfolk home—the
Blunderstone rookery, where there were no rooks—are
among the most beautiful pictures of childhood in existence. In what sunshine of love does the lad bask with
his mother and Peggotty, till Mrs. Copperfield contracts
her disastrous second marriage with Mr. Murdstone !
Then how the scene changes. There come harshness and
cruelty ; banishment to Mr. Creakle's villainous school ;
the poor mother's death ; the worse banishment to London,
and descent into warehouse drudgery ; the strange shabby-
genteel, happy-go-lucky life with the Micawbers ; the
flight from intolerable ills in the forlorn hope that David's
aunt will take pity on him. Here the scene changes
again. Miss Betsy Trotwood, a fine old gnarled piece of
womanhood, places the boy at school at Canterbury,
where he makes acquaintance with Agnes, the woman
whom he marries far, far on in the story ; and with her
father, Mr. Wickham, a somewhat port wine-loving lawyer ;
and with Uriah Heep, the fawning villain of the piece.
How David is first articled to a proctor in Doctors' Commons, and then becomes a reporter, and then a successful
author ; and how he marries his first wife, the childish
Dora, who dies ; and how, meanwhile, Uriah is effecting
the general ruin, and aspiring to the hand of Agnes, till
his villanies are detected and his machinations defeated
by Micawber—how all this comes about, would be a long
story to tell. But, as is usual with Dickens, there are
subsidiary rills of story running into the main stream, and
by one of these I should like to linger a moment. The
head-boy, and a kind of parlour-boarder, at Mr. Creakles'

establishment, is one Steerforth, the spoilt only son of a widow. This Steerforth, David meets again when both are young men, and they go down together to Yarmouth, and there David is the means of making him known to a family of fisherfolk. He is rich, handsome, with an indescribable charm, according to his friends' testimony, and he induces the fisherman's niece, the pretty Em'ly, to desert her home, and the young boat-builder to whom she is engaged, and to fly to Italy. Now to this story, as Dickens tells it, French criticism objects that he dwells exclusively on the sin and sorrow, and sets aside that in which the French novelist would delight, viz., the mad force and irresistible sway of passion. To which English criticism may, I think, reply, that the "pity of it," the wide-working desolation, are as essentially part of such an event as the passion ; and, therefore, even from an exclusively artistic point of view, just as fit subjects for the novelist.

While "David Copperfield" was in progress, Dickens started on a new venture. He had often before projected a periodical, and twice, as we have seen,—once in *Master Humphrey's Clock*, and again as editor of *The Daily News*,—had attempted quasi-journalism or its reality. But now at last he had struck the right vein. He had discovered a means of utilizing his popularity, and imparting it to a paper, without being under the crushing necessity of writing the whole of that paper himself. The first number of *Household Words* appeared on the 30th of March, 1850.

The "preliminary word" heralds the paper in thoroughly characteristic fashion, and is, not unnaturally, far more

personal in tone than the first leading article of the first
number of *The Daily News*, though that, too, be it said
in passing, bears traces, through all its officialism, of
having come from the same pen.[1] In introducing *Household Words* to his new readers, Dickens speaks feelingly,
eloquently, of his own position as a writer, and the responsibilities attached to his popularity, and tells of his hope
that a future of instruction, and amusement, and kindly
playful fancy may be in store for the paper. Nor were
his happy anticipations belied. All that he had pro-
mised, he gave. *Household Words* found an entrance
into innumerable homes, and was everywhere recognized
as a friend. Never did editor more strongly impress his
own personality upon his staff. The articles were sprightly,
amusing, interesting, and instructive too—often very instructive, but always in an interesting way. That was one
of the periodical's main features. The pill of knowledge
was always presented gilt. Taking *Household Words* and
All the Year Round together—and for this purpose they
may properly be regarded as one and the same paper,
because the change of name and proprietorship in 1859[2]
brought no change in form or character,—taking them
together, I say, they contain a vast quantity of very
pleasant, if not very profound, reading. Even apart
from the stories, one can do very much worse than while
away an hour, now and again, in gleaning here and there

[1] As, for instance, in such expressions as this : "The stamp on
newspapers is not like the stamp on universal medicine bottles,
which licenses anything, however false and monstrous."

[2] The last number of *Household Words* appeared on the 28th of
May, 1859, and the first of *All the Year Round* on the 30th of April,
1859.

among their pages. Among Dickens' own contributions
may be mentioned "The Child's History of England," and
" Lazy Tour of Two Idle Apprentices "—being the record
of an excursion made by him in 1857, with Mr. Wilkie
Collins ; and " The Uncommercial Traveller" papers.
While as to stories, " Hard Times " appeared in *Household Words ;* and "The Tale of Two Cities " and "Great
Expectations," in *All the Year Round.* And to the Christmas numbers he gave some of his best and daintiest work.
Nor were novels and tales by other competent hands
wanting. Here it was that Mrs. Gaskell gave to the
world those papers on " Cranford " that are so full of a
dainty, delicate humour, and " My Lady Ludlow," and
" North and South," and " A Dark Night's Work."
Here, too, Mr. Wilkie Collins wove together his ingenious threads of plot and mystery in " The Moon-
stone," " The Woman in White," and " No Name." And
here also Lord Lytton published " A Strangé Story," and
Charles Reade his " Very Hard Cash."

The year 1851 opened sadly for Dickens. His
wife, who had been confined of a daughter in the pre-
ceding August, was so seriously unwell that he had to
take her to Malvern. His father, to whom, notwithstanding the latter's peculiarities and eccentricities, he
was greatly attached, died on the 31st of March ; and
on the 14th of April his infant daughter died also. In
connection with this latter death there occurred an incident of great pathos. Dickens had come up from
Malvern on the 14th, to take the chair at the dinner on
behalf of the Theatrical Fund, and looking in at Devonshire Terrace on his way, played with the children, as

was his wont, and fondled the baby, and then went on to the London Tavern.[1] Shortly after he left the house, the child died, suddenly. The news was communicated to Forster, who was also at the dinner, and he decided that it would be better not to tell the poor father till the speech of the evening had been made. So Dickens made his speech, and a brilliant one it was—it is brilliant even as one reads it now, in the coldness of print, without the glamour of the speaker's voice, and presence, and yet brilliant with an undertone of sadness, which the recent death of the speaker's father would fully explain. And Forster, who knew of the yet later blow impending on his friend, had to sit by and listen as that dear friend, all unconscious of the dread application of the words, spoke of "the actor" having "sometimes to come from scenes of sickness, of suffering, ay, even of death itself, to play his part ;" and then went on to tell how "all of us, in our spheres, have as often to do violence to our feelings, and to hide our hearts in fighting this great battle of life, and in discharging our duties and responsibilities."

In this same year, 1851, Dickens left the house in Devonshire Terrace, now grown too small for his enlarging household, and, after a long sojourn at Broadstairs, moved into Tavistock House, in Tavistock Square. Here "Bleak House" was begun at the end of November, the first number being published in the ensuing March. It is a fine work of art unquestionably, a very fine work of art—the canvas all crowded with living figures, and yet

[1] There are one or two slight discrepancies between Forster's narrative and that of Miss Dickens and Miss Hogarth. The latter are clearly more likely to be right on such a matter.

the main lines of the composition well-ordered and harmonious. Two threads of interest run through the story,
one following the career of Lady Dedlock, and the other
tracing the influence of a great Chancery suit on the
victims immeshed in its toils. From the first these two
threads are distinct, and yet happily interwoven. Let us
take Lady Dedlock's thread first. She is the wife of Sir
Leicester Dedlock, whose "family is as old as the hills,
and a great deal more respectable," and she is still very
beautiful, though no longer in the bloom of youth, and
she is cold and haughty of manner, as a woman of highest
fashion sometimes may be. But in her past there is an
ugly hidden secret ; and a girl of sweetest disposition walks
her kindly course through the story, who might call Lady
Dedlock "mother." This secret, or perhaps rather the
fact that there is a secret at all, she reveals in a moment
of surprise to the family lawyer; and she lays herself
still further open to his suspicions by going, disguised in
her maid's clothes, to the poor graveyard where her former
lover lies buried. The lawyer worms the whole story out,
and, just as he is going to reveal it, is murdered by the
French maid aforesaid. But the murder comes too late
to save my lady, nay, adds to her difficulties. She flies,
in anticipation of the disclosure of her secret, and is found
dead at the graveyard gate. To such end has the sin of
her youth led her. So once again has Dickens dwelt, not
on the passionate side of wrongful love, but on its sorrow.
Now take the other thread—the Chancery suit—"Jarndyce
versus Jarndyce," a suit held in awful reverence by the
profession as a "monument of Chancery practice"—a
suit seemingly interminable, till, after long, long years of

wrangling and litigation, the fortuitous discovery of a will
settles it all, with the result that the whole estate has been
swallowed up in the costs. And how about the litigants?
How about poor Richard Carstone and his wife, whom we
see, in the opening of the story, in all the heyday and
happiness of their youth, strolling down to the court—
they are its wards,—and wondering sadly over the "head-
ache and heartache" of it all, and then saying, gleefully,
"at all events Chancery will work none of its bad influence on *us*"? "None of its bad influence on *us*!"
poor lad, whose life is wasted and character impaired in
following the mirage of the suit, and who is killed by the
mockery of its end. Thus do the two intertwined stories
run ; but apart from these, though all in place and keeping, and helping on the general development, there is a
whole profusion of noticeable characters. In enume-
rating them, however baldly, one scarcely knows where
to begin. The lawyer group—clerks and all—is excellent. Dickens' early experiences stood him in good stead
here. Excellent too are those studies in the ways of impecuniosity and practical shiftlessness, Harold Skimpole,
the airy, irresponsible, light-hearted epicurean, with his
pretty tastes and dilettante accomplishments, and Mrs.
Jellyby, the philanthropist, whose eyes "see nothing
nearer" than Borrioboola-Gha, on the banks of the far
Niger, and never dwell to any purpose on the utter
discomfort of the home of her husband and children.
Characters of this kind no one ever delineated better
than Dickens. That Leigh Hunt, the poet and essayist,
who had sat for the portrait of Skimpole, was not
altogether flattered by the likeness, is comprehensible

enough; and in truth it is unfair, both to painter
and model, that we should take such portraits too
seriously. Landor, who sat for the thunderous and kindly
Boythorn, had more reason to be satisfied. Besides
these one may mention Joe, the outcast ; and Mr. Turvey-
drop, the beau of the school of the Regency—how horrified
he would have been at the juxtaposition—and George,
the keeper of the rifle gallery, a fine soldierly figure ; and
Mr. Bucket, the detective—though Dickens had a tendency to idealize the abilities of the police force. As
to Sir Leicester Dedlock, I think he is, on the whole,
"mine author's " best study of the aristocracy, a direction
in which Dickens' forte did not lie, for Sir Leicester *is* a
gentleman, and receives the terrible blow that falls upon
him in a spirit at once chivalrous and human.

What between " Bleak House," *Household Words*,
and "The Child's History of England," Dickens, in the
spring of 1853, was overworked and ill. Brighton failed
to restore him ; and he took his family over to Boulogne
in June, occupying there a house belonging to a certain
M. de Beaucourt. Town, dwelling, and landlord, all
suited him exactly. Boulogne he declared to be admirable for its picturesqueness in buildings and life, and
equal in some respects to Naples itself. The dwelling, "a
doll's house of many rooms," embowered in roses, and
with a terraced garden, was a place after his own heart.
While as to the landlord—he was " wonderful." Dickens
never tires of extolling his virtues, his generosity, his
kindness, his anxiety to please, his pride in " the
property." All the pleasant delicate quaint traits in
the man's character are irradiated as if with French sun-

shine in his tenant's description. It is a dainty little picture and painted with the kindliest of brushes. Poor Beaucourt, he was "inconsolable" when he and Dickens finally parted three years afterwards—for twice again did the latter occupy a house, but not this same house, on " the property." Many were the tears that he shed, and even the garden, the loved garden, went forlorn and un-weeded. But that was in 1856. The parting was not so final and terrible in the October of 1853, when Dickens, having finished "Bleak House," started with Mr. Wilkie Collins, and Augustus Egg, the artist, for a holiday tour in Switzerland and Italy.

CHAPTER X.

O N his return to England, just after the Christmas of 1853, Dickens gave his first public readings. He had, as we have seen, read "The Chimes" some nine years before, to a select few among his literary friends ; and at Lausanne he had similarly read portions of "Dombey and Son." But the three readings given at Birmingham, on the 27th, 29th, and 30th December, 1853, were, in every sense, public entertainments, and, except that the proceeds were devoted entirely to the local Institute, differed in no way from the famous readings by which he afterwards realized what may almost be called a fortune. The idea of coming before the world in this new character had long been in his mind. As early as 1846, after the private reading at Lausanne, he had written to Forster : "I was thinking the other day that in these days of lecturings and readings, a great deal of money might possibly be made (if it were not *infra dig.*) by one's having readings of one's own books. I think it would take immensely. What do you say?" Forster said then, and said consistently throughout, that he held the thing to be "*infra dig.*," and unworthy of Dickens' position ;

and in this I think one may venture to assert that Forster was wrong. There can surely be no reason why a popular writer, who happens also to be an excellent elocutionist, should not afford general pleasure by giving sound to his prose, and a voice to his imaginary characters. Nor is it opposed to the fitness of things that he should be paid for his skill. If, however, one goes further in Dickens' case, and asks whether the readings did not involve too great an expenditure of time, energy, and, as we shall see, ultimately of life, and whether he would not, in the highest sense, have been better employed over his books, —why then the question becomes more difficult of solution. But, after all, each man must answer such questions for himself. Dickens may have felt, as the years began to tell, that he required the excitement of the readings for mental stimulus, and that he would not even have written as much as he did without them. Be that as it may, the success at Birmingham, where a sum of from £400 to £500 was realized, the requests that poured in upon him to read at other places, the invariably renewed success whenever he did so, the clear evidence that a large sum was to be realized if he determined to come forward on his own account, all must have contributed to scatter Forster's objections to the winds. On the 29th of April, 1858, at St. Martin's Hall, in London, he started his career as a paid public reader, and he continued to read, with shorter or longer periods of intermission, till his death. But into the story of his professional tours it is not my intention just now to enter. I shall only stay to say a few words about the character and quality of his readings.

That they were a success can readily be accounted for. The mere desire to see and hear Dickens, the great Dickens, the novelist who was more than popular, who was the object of real personal affection on the part of the English-speaking race,—this would have drawn a crowd at any time. But Dickens was not the man to rely upon such sources of attraction, any more than an actress who is really an actress will consent to rely exclusively on her good looks. " Whatever is worth doing at all is worth doing well," such as we have seen was one of the governing principles of his life ; and he read very well. Of nervousness there was no trace in his composition. To some one who asked him whether he ever felt any shyness as a speaker, he answered, " Not in the least ; the first time I took the chair (at a public dinner) I felt as much confidence as if I had done the thing a hundred times." This of course helped him much as a reader, and gave him full command over all his gifts. But the gifts were also assiduously cultivated. He laboured, one might almost say, agonized, to make himself a master of the art. Mr. Dolby, who acted as his " manager," during the tours undertaken from 1866 to 1870, tells us that before producing " Dr. Marigold," he not only gave a kind of semi-public rehearsal, but had rehearsed it to himself considerably over two hundred times. Writing to Forster Dickens says : " You have no idea how I have worked at them [the readings] . . . I have tested all the serious passion in them by everything I know, made the humorous points much more humorous ; corrected my utterance of certain words ; . . . I learnt " Dombey " like the rest, and did it to myself often twice a day, with exactly the same pains as at night, over, and over, and over again."

The results justified the care and effort bestowed. There are, speaking generally, two schools of readers : those who dramatize what they read, and those who read simply, audibly, with every attention to emphasis and point, but with no effort to do more than slightly indicate differences of personage or character. To the latter school Thackeray belonged. He read so as to be perfectly heard, and perfectly understood, and so that the innate beauty of his literary style might have full effect. Dickens read quite differently. He read not as a writer to whom style is everything, but as an actor throwing himself into the world he wished to bring before his hearers. He was so careless indeed of pure literature, in this particular matter, that he altered his books for the readings, eliminating much of the narrative, and emphasizing the dialogue. He was pre-eminently the dramatic reader. Carlyle, who had been dragged to " Hanover Rooms," to "the complete upsetting," as he says, " of my evening habitudes, and spiritual composure," was yet constrained to declare : " Dickens does it capitally, such as *it* is ; acts better than any Macready in the world ; a whole tragic, comic, heroic, *theatre* visible, performing under one *hat*, and keeping us laughing—in a sorry way, some of us thought—the whole night. He is a good creature, too, and makes fifty or sixty pounds by each of these readings." "A whole theatre "—that is just the right expression minted for us by the great coiner of phrases. Dickens, by mere play of voice, for the gestures were comparatively sober,

placed before you, on his imaginary stage, the men and
women he had created. There Dr. Marigold pattered
his cheap-jack phrases ; and Mrs. Gamp and Betsy Prig,
with throats rendered husky by much gin, had their
memorable quarrel ; and Sergeant Buzfuz bamboozled
that stupid jury ; and Boots at the Swan told his pretty
tale of child-elopement ; and Fagin, in his hoarse Jew
whisper, urged Bill Sikes to his last foul deed of murder.
Ay me, in the great hush of the past there are tones of
the reader's voice that still linger in my ears ! I seem to
hear once more the agonized quick utterance of poor
Nancy, as she pleads for life, and the dread stillness after
the ruffian's cruel blows have fallen on her upturned face.
Again comes back to me the break in Bob Cratchit's
voice, as he speaks of the death of Tiny Tim. As of old
I listen to poor little Chops, the dwarf, declaring, very
piteously, that his " fashionable friends " don't use him
well, and put him on the mantel-piece when he refuses to
"have in more champagne-wine," and lock him in the
sideboard when he " won't give up his property." And
I *see*—yes, I declare I *see*, as I saw when Dickens was
reading, such was the illusion of voice and gesture—that
dying flame of Scrooge's fire, which leaped up when
Marley's ghost came in, and then fell again. Nor can I
forbear to mention, among these reminiscences, that there
is also a passage in one of Thackeray's lectures that is
still in my ears as on the evening when I heard it. It is
a passage in which he spoke of the love that children had
for the works of his more popular rival, and told how his
own children would come to him and ask, " Why don't
you write books like Mr. Dickens ? "

CHAPTER XI.

CHANCERY had occupied a prominent place in "Bleak House." Philosophical radicalism occupied the same kind of position in "Hard Times," which was commenced in the number of *Household Words* for the 1st of April, 1854. The book, when afterwards published in a complete form, bore a dedication to Carlyle ; and very fittingly so, for much of its philosophy is his. Dickens, like Kingsley, and like Mr. Ruskin and Mr. Froude, and so many other men of genius and ability, had come under the influence of the old Chelsea sage.[1] And what are the ideas which "Hard Times" is thus intended to popularize? These : that men are not merely intellectual calculating machines, with reason and self-interest for motive power, but creatures possessing also affections, feelings, fancy—a whole world of emotions that lie outside the ken of the older school of political economists. Therefore, to imagine that they can live and flourish on facts alone is a fallacy and pernicious ; as is also the notion that any human relations can be

---

[1] Dickens did not accept the whole Carlyle creed. He retained a sort of belief in the collective wisdom of the people, which Carlyle certainly did not share. .

permanently established on a basis of pure supply and
demand. If we add to this an unlimited contempt for
Parliament, as a place where the national dustmen are
continually stirring the national dust to no purpose at
all, why then we are pretty well advanced in the philosophy of Carlyle. And how does Dickens illustrate these
points? ⌈We are at Coketown, a place, as its name
implies, of smoke and manufacture. Here lives and
flourishes Thomas Gradgrind, "a man of realities; a man
of facts and calculations;" not essentially a bad man,
but bound in an iron system as in a vice. He brings up
his children on knowledge, and enlightened self-interest
exclusively; and the boy becomes a cub and a mean
thief, and the girl marries, quite without love, a certain
blustering Mr. Bounderby, and is as nearly as possible led
astray by the first person who approaches her with the
language of gallantry and sentiment.⌋ Mr. Bounderby, her
husband, is, one may add, a man who, in mere lying
bounce, makes out his humble origin to be more humble
than it is. On the other side of the picture are Mr.
Sleary and his circus troupe; and Cissy Jupe, the
daughter of the clown; and the almost saintly figures of
Stephen Blackpool, and Rachel, a working man and a
working woman. With these people facts are as naught,
and self-interest as dust in the balance. Mr. Sleary has
a heart which no brandy-and-water can harden, and he
enables Mr. Gradgrind to send off the wretched cub to
America, refusing any guerdon but a glass of his favourite
beverage. The circus troupe are kindly, simple, loving
folk. Cissy Jupe proves the angel of the Gradgrind
household. ⌈Stephen is the victim of unjust persecution

on the part of his own class, is suspected, by young Gradgrind's machinations, of the theft committed by that young scoundrel, falls into a disused pit as he is coming to vindicate his character, and only lives long enough to forgive his wrongs, and clasp in death the hand of Rachel—a hand which in life could not be his, as he had a wife alive who was a drunkard and worse. A marked contrast, is it not? On one side all darkness, and on the other all light. The demons of fact and self-interest opposed to the angels of fancy and unselfishness. A contrast too violent unquestionably. Exaggeration is the fault of the novel. One may at once allow, for instance, that Rachel and Stephen, though human nature in its infinite capacity may include such characters, are scarcely a typical working woman and working man. But then neither, heaven be praised, are Coupeau the sot, and Gervaise the drab, in M. Zola's "Drink"—and, for my part, I think Rachel and Stephen the better company.

"Sullen socialism"—such is Macaulay's view of the political philosophy of "Hard Times." "Entirely right in main drift and purpose"—such is the verdict of Mr. Ruskin. Who shall decide between the two? or, if a decision be necessary, then I would venture to say, yes, entirely right in feeling. Dickens is right in sympathy for those who toil and suffer, right in desire to make their lives more human and beautiful, right in belief that the same human heart beats below all class distinctions. But, beyond this, a novelist only, not a philosopher, not fitted to grapple effectively with complex social and political problems, and to solve them to right conclusions.

There are some things unfortunately which even the best and kindest instincts cannot accomplish.

The last chapter of "Hard Times" appeared in the number of *Household Words* for the 12th of August, 1854, and the first number of "Little Dorrit" came out at Christmas, 1855. Between those dates a great war had waxed and waned. The heart of England had been terribly moved by the story of the sufferings and privations which the army had had to undergo amid the snows of a Russian winter. From the trenches before Sebastopol the newspaper correspondents had sent terrible accounts of death and disease, and of ills which, as there seemed room for suspicion, might have been prevented by better management. Through long disuse the army had rusted in its scabbard, and everything seemed to go wrong but the courage of officers and men. A great demand arose for reform in the whole administration of the country. A movement, now much forgotten, though not fruitless at the time, was started for the purpose of making the civil service more efficient, and putting John Bull's house in order. "Administrative Reform," such was the cry of the moment, and Dickens uttered it with the full strength of his lungs. He attended a great meeting held at Drury Lane Theatre on the 27th of June, in furtherance of the cause, and made what he declared to be his first political speech. He spoke on the subject again at the dinner of the Theatrical Fund. He urged on his friends in the press to the attack. He was in the forefront of the battle. And when his next novel, " Little Dorrit," appeared, there was the Civil Service, like a sort of gibbeted Punch, executing the strangest antics.

9

But the " Circumlocution Office," where the clerks sit lazily devising all day long "how *not* to do" the business of the country, and devote their energies alternately to marmalade and general insolence,—the " Circumlocution Office " occupies after all only a secondary position in the book. The main interest of it circles round the place that had at one time been almost a home to Dickens. Again he drew upon his earlier experiences. We are once more introduced into a debtors' prison. Little Dorrit is the child of the Marshalsea, born and bred within its walls, the sole living thing about the place on which its taint does not fall. Her worthless brother, her sister, her father—who is not only her father, but the "father of the Marshalsea " —the prison blight is on all three. Her father especially is a piece of admirable character-drawing. Dickens has often been accused of only catching the surface peculiarities of his personages, their outward tricks, and obvious habits of speech and of mind. Such a study as Mr. Dorrit would alone be sufficient to rebut the charge. No novelist specially famed for dissecting character to its innermost recesses could exhibit a finer piece of mental analysis. We follow the poor weak creature's deterioration from the time when the helpless muddle in his affairs brings him into durance. We note how his sneaking pride seems to feed even on the garbage of his degradation. We see how little inward change there is in the man himself when there comes a transformation scene in his fortunes, and he leaves the Marshalsea wealthy and prosperous. It is all thoroughly worked out, perfect, a piece of really great art. No wonder that Mr. Clennam pities the child of such a father; indeed, considering what a really admirable woman she is, one only wonders that his pity does not sooner turn to love.

"Little Dorrit" ran its course from December, 1855, to June, 1857, and within that space of time there occurred two or three incidents in Dickens' career which should not pass unnoticed. At the first of these dates he was in Paris, where he remained till the middle of May, 1856, greatly fêted by the French world of letters and art; dining hither and thither; now enjoying an Arabian Nights sort of banquet given by Emile de Girardin, the popular journalist; now meeting George Sand, the great novelist, whom he describes as "just the sort of woman in appearance whom you might suppose to be the queen's monthly nurse—chubby, matronly, swarthy, black-eyed;" then studying French art, and contrasting it with English art, somewhat to the disadvantage of the latter; anon superintending the translation of his works into French, and working hard at " Little Dorrit ;" and all the while frequenting the Paris theatres with great assiduity and admiration. Meanwhile, too, on the 14th of March, 1856, a Friday, his lucky day as he considered it, he had written a cheque for the purchase of Gad's Hill Place, at which he had so often looked when a little lad, living penuriously at Chatham—the house which it had been the object of his childish ambition to win for his own.

So had merit proved to be not without its visible prize, literally a prize for good conduct. He took possession of the house in the following February, and turned workmen into it, and finished "Little Dorrit" there. At first the purchase was intended mainly as an investment, and he only purposed to spend some portion of his time at Gad's Hill, letting it at other periods, and so recouping himself for the interest on the £1,790 which it had cost, and for the further sums which he expended on improvements. But as time went on it became his hobby, the love of his advancing years. He beautified here and beautified there, built a new drawing-room, added bedrooms, constructed a tunnel under the road, erected in the "wilderness" on the other side of the road a Swiss châlet, which had been presented to him by Fechter, the French-English actor, and in short indulged in all the thousand and one vagaries of a proprietor who is enamoured of his property. The matter seems to have been one of the family jokes; and when, on the Sunday before his death, he showed the conservatory to his younger daughter, and said, "Well, Katey, now you see *positively* the last improvement at Gad's Hill," there was a general laugh. But this is far on in the story; and very long before the building of the conservatory, long indeed before the main other changes had been made, the idea of an investment had been abandoned. In 1860 he sold Tavistock House, in London, and made Gad's Hill Place his final home.

Even here, however, I am anticipating; for before getting to 1860 there is in Dickens' history a page which one would willingly turn over, if that were possible, in silence and sadness. But it is not possible. No account of his life would be complete, and what is of more importance, true, if it made no mention of his relations with his wife.

For some time before 1858 Dickens had been in an

over-excited, nervous, morbid state. During earlier manhood his animal spirits and fresh energy had been superb.
Now, as the years advanced, and especially at this particular time, the energy was the same ; but it was accompanied by something of feverishness and disease. He
could not be quiet. In the autumn of 1857 he wrote to
Forster, " I have now no relief but in action. I am
become incapable of rest. I am quite confident I
should rust, break, and die if I spared myself. Much
better to die doing." And again, a little later, " If I
couldn't walk fast and far, I should just explode and
perish." It was the foreshadowing of such utterances
as these, and the constant wanderings to and fro for
readings and theatricals and what not, that led Harriet
Martineau, who had known and greatly liked Dickens, to
say after perusing the second volume of his life, " I am
much struck by his hysterical restlessness. It must have
been terribly wearing to his wife." On the other hand,
there can be no manner of doubt that his wife wore
him. " Why is it," he had said to Forster in one of the
letters from which I have just quoted, " that, as with poor
David (Copperfield), a sense comes always crushing on
me now, when I fall into low spirits, as of one happiness
I have missed in life, and one friend and companion I
have never made ? " And again : " I find that the
skeleton in my domestic closet is becoming a pretty
big one." Then come even sadder confidences : " Poor
Catherine and I are not made for each other, and there
is no help for it. It is not only that she makes me
uneasy and unhappy, but that I make her so too, and
much more so. She is exactly what you know in the way

of being amiable and complying; but we are strangely ill-assorted for the bond there is between us. . . . Her temperament will not go with mine." And at last, in March, 1858, two months before the end : " It is not with me a matter of will, or trial, or sufferance, or good humour, or making the best of it, or making the worst of it, any longer. It is all despairingly over." So, after living together for twenty years, these two went their several ways in May, 1858. Dickens allowed to his wife an income of £600 a year, and the eldest son went to live with her. The other children and their aunt, Miss Hogarth, remained with Dickens himself.

Scandal has not only a poisonous, but a busy tongue, and when a well-known public man and his wife agree to live apart, the beldame seldom neglects to give her special version of the affair. So it happened here. Some miserable rumour was whispered about to the detriment of Dickens' morals. He was at the time, as we have seen, in an utterly morbid, excited state, sore doubtless with himself, and altogether out of mental condition, and the lie stung him almost to madness. He published an article branding it as it deserved in the number of *Household Words* for the 12th of June, 1858.

So far his course of action was justifiable. Granted that it was judicious to notice the rumour at all, and to make his private affairs the matter of public comment, then there was nothing in the terms of the article to which objection could be taken. It contained no reflection of any kind on Mrs. Dickens. It was merely an honest man's indignant protest against an anonymous libel which implicated others as well as himself. Whether

the publication, however, was judicious is a different
matter. Forster thinks not. He holds that Dickens had
altogether exaggerated the public importance of the
rumour, and the extent of its circulation. And this,
according to my own recollection, is entirely true. I
was a lad at the time, but a great lover of Dickens'
works, as most lads then were, and I well remember
the feeling of surprise and regret which that article
created among us of the general public. At the
same time, it is only fair to Dickens to recollect that
the lying story was, at least, so far fraught with danger to
his reputation, that Mrs. Dickens would seem for a time
to have believed it ; and further, that Dickens occupied a
very peculiar position towards the public, and a position
that might well in his own estimation, and even in ours,
give singular importance to the general belief in his
personal character.

This point will bear dwelling upon. Dickens claimed,
and claimed truly, that the relation between himself and
the public was one of exceptional sympathy and affection. Perhaps an illustration will best show what that
kind of relationship was. Thackeray tells of two ladies
with whom he had, at different times, discussed " The
Christmas Carol," and how each had concluded by
saying of the author, "God bless him ! ". God bless him !
—that was the sort of feeling towards himself which
Dickens had succeeded in producing in most English
hearts. He had appealed from the first and so constantly
to every kind and gentle emotion, had illustrated so often
what is good and true in human character, had pleaded
the cause of the weak and suffering with such assiduity,

had been so scathingly indignant at all wrong ; and he had moreover shown such a manly and chivalrous purity in all his utterance with regard to women, that his readers felt for him a kind of personal tenderness, quite distinct from their mere admiration for his genius as a writer. Nor was that feeling based on his books alone. So far as one could learn at the time, no great dissimilarity existed between the author and the man. We all remember Byron's corrosive remark on the sentimentalist Sterne, that he " whined over a dead ass, and allowed his mother to die of hunger." But Dickens' feelings were by no means confined to his pen. He was known to be a good father and a good friend, and of perfect truth and honesty. The kindly tolerance for the frailties of a father or brother which he admired in Little Dorrit, he was ready to extend to his own father and his own brother. He was most assiduous in the prosecution of his craft as a writer, and yet had time and leisure of heart at command for all kinds of good and charitable work. His private character had so far stood above all floating cloud of suspicion.

That Dickens felt an honourable pride in the general affection he inspired, can readily be understood. He also felt, even more honourably, its great responsibility. He knew that his books and he himself were a power for good, and he foresaw how greatly his influence would suffer if a suspicion of hypocrisy—the vice at which he had always girded—were to taint his reputation. Here, for instance, in " Little Dorrit," the work written in the thick of his home troubles, he had written of Clennam as " a man who had, deep-rooted in his nature, a belief in all the gentle and good things his life had been without," and

had shown how this belief had "saved Clennam still from
the whimpering weakness and cruel selfishness of holding
that because such a happiness or such a virtue had not
come into his little path, or worked well for him, therefore
it was not in the great scheme, but was reducible, when
found in appearance, to the basest elements." A touching
utterance if it expressed the real feeling of a writer sorely
disappointed and in great trouble; but an utterance
moving rather to contempt if it came from a writer who
had transferred his affections from his wife to some other
woman. I do not wonder, therefore, that Dickens,
excited and exasperated, spoke out, though I think it
would have been better if he had kept silence.

But he did other things that were not justifiable. He
quarrelled with Messrs. Bradbury and Evans, his publishers, because they did not use their influence to get
Punch, a periodical in which Dickens had no interest,
to publish the personal statement that had appeared in
Household Words; and worse, much worse, he wrote a
letter, which ought never to have been written, detailing
the grounds on which he and his wife had separated. This
letter, dated the 28th of May, 1858, was addressed to his
secretary, Arthur Smith, and was to be shown to any one
interested. Arthur Smith showed it to the London cor-
respondent of *The New York Tribune,* who naturally
caused it to be published in that paper. Then Dickens
was horrified. He was a man of far too high and chivalrous feeling not to know that the letter contained statements with regard to his wife's failings which ought never
to have been made public. He knew as well as any one,
that a literary man ought not to take the world into

his confidence on such a subject. Ever afterwards he referred to the letter as his "violated letter." But, in truth, the wrong went deeper than the publication. The letter should never have been written, certainly never sent to Arthur Smith for general perusal. Dickens' only excuse is the fact that he was clearly not himself at the time, and that he never fell into a like error again. It is, however, sad to notice how entirely his wife seems to have passed out of his affection. The reference to her in his will is almost unkind; and when death was on him she seems not to have been summoned to his bedside.

CHAPTER XII.

DICKENS' career as a reader reading for money commenced on the 29th of April, 1858, while the trouble about his wife was at the thickest; and, after reading in London on sixteen nights, he made a reading tour in the provinces, and in Scotland and Ireland. In the following year he read likewise. But meanwhile, which is more important to us than his readings, he was writing another book. On the 30th of April, 1859, in the first number of *All the Year Round*,[1] was begun "The Tale of Two Cities," a simultaneous publication in monthly parts being also commenced.

"The Tale of Two Cities" is a tale of the great French Revolution of 1793, and the two cities in question are London and Paris,—London as it lay comparatively at peace in the days when George III. was king, and Paris running blood and writhing in the fierce fire of anarchy and mob rule. A powerful book, unquestionably. No doubt there is in its heat and glare a reflection from Carlyle's "French Revolution," a book for which Dickens had the greatest admiration. But that need not be re-

[1] His foolish quarrel with Bradbury and Evans had necessitated the abandonment of *Household Words.*

garded as a demerit. Dickens is no pale copyist, and
adds fervour to what he borrows. His pictures of Paris
in revolution are as fine as the London scenes in "Barnaby Rudge;" and the interweaving of the story with
public events is even better managed in the later book
than in the earlier story of the Gordon riots. And the
story, what does it tell? It tells of a certain Dr. Manette,
who, after long years of imprisonment in the Bastile, is
restored to his daughter in London; and of a young
French noble, who has assumed the name of Darnay, and
left France in horror of the doings of his order, and who
marries Dr. Manette's daughter; and of a young English
barrister, able enough in his profession, but careless of
personal success, and much addicted to port wine, and
bearing a striking personal resemblance to the young
French noble. These persons, and others, being drawn to
Paris by various strong inducements, Darnay is condemned
to death as a *ci-devant* noble, and the ne'er-do-weel barrister, out of the great pure love he bears to Darnay's wife,
succeeds in dying for him. That is the tale's bare outline; and if any one says of the book that it is in parts
melodramatic, one may fitly answer that never was any
portion of the world's history such a thorough piece of
melodrama as the French Revolution.

With "The Tale of Two Cities" Hablôt K. Browne's
connection with Dickens, as the illustrator of his books,
came to an end. The "Sketches" had been illustrated by
Cruikshank, who was the great popular illustrator of the
time, and it is amusing to read, in the preface to the first
edition of the first series, published in 1836, how the
trembling young author placed himself, as it were, under

the protection of the "well-known individual who had frequently contributed to the success of similar undertakings." Cruikshank also illustrated "Oliver Twist;" and indeed, with an arrogance which unfortunately is not incompatible with genius, afterwards set up a rather preposterous claim to have been the real originator of that book, declaring that he had worked out the story in a series of etchings, and that Dickens had illustrated *him*, and not he Dickens.[1] But apart from the drawings for the "Sketches" and "Oliver Twist," and the first few drawings by Seymour, and two drawings by Buss,[2] in "Pickwick," and some drawings by Cattermole in *Master Humphrey's Clock*, and by Samuel Palmer in the "Pictures from Italy," and by various hands in the Christmas stories—apart from these, Browne, or "Phiz," had executed the illustrations to Dickens' novels. Nor, with all my admiration for certain excellent qualities which his work undeniably possessed, do I think that this was altogether a good thing. Such, I know, is not a popular opinion. But I confess I am unable to agree with those critics who, from their remarks on the recent jubilee edition of "Pickwick," seem to think his illustrations so pre-eminently fine that they should be permanently associated with Dickens' stories. The editor of that edition was, in my view, quite right in treating Browne's illustrations as practically obsolete. The value of Dickens' works is perennial, and Browne's illustrations

[1] See his pamphlet, "The Artist and the Author." The matter is fully discussed in his life by Mr. Blanchard Jerrold.

[2] Buss's illustrations were executed under great disadvantages, and are bad. Those of Seymour are excellent.

represent the art fashion of a time only. So, too, I am unable to see any great cause to regret that Cruikshank's artistic connection with Dickens came to an end so soon.[1] For both Browne and Cruikshank were pre-eminently caricaturists, and caricaturists of an old school. The latter had no idea of beauty. His art, very great art in its way, was that of grotesqueness and exaggeration. He never drew a lady or gentleman in his life. And though Browne, in my view much the lesser artist, was superior in these respects to Cruikshank, yet he too drew the most hideous Pecksniffs, and Tom Pinches, and Joey B.'s, and a whole host of characters quite unreal and absurd. The mischief of it is, too, that Dickens' humour will not bear caricaturing. The defect of his own art as a writer is that it verges itself too often on caricature. Exaggeration is its bane. When, for instance, he makes the rich alderman in "The Chimes" eat up poor Trotty Veck's little last tit-bit of tripe, we are clearly in the region of broad farce. When Mr. Pancks, in "Little Dorrit," so far abandons the ordinary ways of mature rent collectors as to ask a respectable old accountant to. "give him a back," in the Marshalsea court, and leaps over his head, we are obviously in a world of pantomime. Dickens' comic effects are generally quite forced enough, and should never be further forced when translated into the sister art of drawing. Rather, if anything, should they be attenuated. But unfortunately exaggeration happened to be inherent in the draftsmanship of both Cruikshank and Browne.

[1] I am always sorry, however, that Cruikshank did not illustrate the Christmas stories.

And, having said this, I may as well finish with the subject of the illustrations to Dickens' books. "Our Mutual Friend" was illustrated by Mr. Marcus Stone, R.A., then a rising young artist, and the son of Dickens' old friend, Frank Stone. Here the designs fall into the opposite defect. They are, some of them, pretty enough, but they want character. Mr. Fildes' pictures for "Edwin Drood" are a decided improvement. As to the illustrations for the later *Household Edition*, they are very inferior. The designs for a great many are clearly bad, and the mechanical execution almost uniformly so. Even Mr. Barnard's skill has had no fair chance against poor woodcutting, careless engraving, and inferior paper. And this is the more to be regretted, in that Mr. Barnard, by natural affinity of talent, has, to my thinking, done some of the best art work that has been done at all in connection with Dickens. His *Character Sketches*, especially the lithographed series, are admirable. The Jingle is a masterpiece; but all are good, and he even succeeds in making something pictorially acceptable of Little Nell and Little Dorrit.

Just a year, almost to a day, elapsed between the conclusion of "The Tale of Two Cities," and the commencement of "Great Expectations." The last chapter of the former appeared in the number of *All the Year Round* for the 26th of November, 1859, and the first chapter of the latter in the number of the same periodical for the 1st of December, 1860. Poor Pip—for such is the name of the hero of the book—poor Pip, I think he is to be pitied. Certainly he lays himself open to the charge of snobbishness, and is unduly ashamed of his connections.

But then circumstances were decidedly against him. Through some occult means he is removed from his natural sphere, from the care of his "rampageous" sister and of her husband, the good, kind, honest Joe, and taken up to London, and brought up as a gentleman, and started in chambers in Barnard's Inn. All this is done through the instrumentality of Mr. Jaggers, a barrister in highest repute among the criminal brotherhood. But Pip not unnaturally thinks that his unknown benefactress is a certain Miss Havisham, who, having been bitterly wronged in her love affairs, lives in eccentric fashion near his native place, amid the mouldering mementoes of her wedding day. What is his horror when he finds that his education, comfort, and prospects have no more reputable foundation than the bounty of a murderous criminal called Magwitch, who has showered all these benefits upon him from the antipodes, in return for the gift of food and a file when he, Magwitch, was trying to escape from the hulks, and Pip was a little lad. Magwitch, the transported convict, comes back to England, at the peril of his life, to make himself known to Pip, and to have the pleasure of looking at that young gentleman. He is again tracked by the police, and caught, notwithstanding Pip's efforts to get him off, and dies in prison. Pip ultimately, very ultimately, marries a young lady oddly brought up by the queer Miss Havisham, and who turns out to be Magwitch's daughter.

Such, as I have had occasion to say before in speaking of similar analyses, such are the dry bones of the story. Pip's character is well drawn. So is that of Joe. And Mr. Jaggers, the criminal's friend, and his clerk, Wemmick, are striking and full of a grim humour. Miss Havisham and her *protégée,* Estella, whom she educates to be the scourge of men, belong to what may be called the melodramatic side of Dickens' art. They take their place with Mrs. Dombey and with Miss Dartle in "David Copperfield," and Miss Wade in "Little Dorrit"—female characters of a fantastic and haughty type, and quite devoid, Miss Dartle and Miss Wade especially, of either verisimilitude or the milk of human kindness.

"Great Expectations" was completed in August, 1861, and the first number of "Our Mutual Friend" appeared in May, 1864. This was an unusual interval, but the great writer's faculty of invention was beginning to lose its fresh spring and spontaneity. And besides he had not been idle. Though writing no novel, he had been busy enough with readings, and his work on *All the Year Round.* He had also written a short, but very graceful paper[1] on Thackeray, whose death, on the Christmas Eve of 1863, had greatly affected him. Now, however, he again braced himself for one of his greater efforts.

Scarcely, I think, as all will agree, with the old success. In "Our Mutual Friend" he is not at his best. It is a strange complicated story that seems to have some difficulty in unravelling itself: the story of a man who pretends to be dead in order that he may, under a changed name, investigate the character and eligibility of the young woman whom an erratic father has destined to be his bride. A golden-hearted old dust contractor, who hides a will that will give him all that erratic father's property, and disinherit the man aforesaid, and who, to

[1] See *Cornhill Magazine* for February, 1864.

19

crown his virtues, pretends to be a miser in order to
teach the young woman, also aforesaid, how bad it is to be
mercenary, and to induce her to marry the unrecognized
and seemingly penniless son ; their marriage accordingly, with ultimate result that the bridegroom turns out
to be no poor clerk, but the original heir, who, of course,
is not dead, and is the inheritor of thousands ; subsidiary
groups of characters, of course, one which I think
rather uninteresting, of some brand-new people called
the Veneerings and their acquaintances, for they have
no friends ; and some fine sketches of the river-side
population ; striking and amusing characters too—Silas
Wegg, the scoundrelly vendor of songs, who ferrets
among the dust for wills in order to confound the good
dustman, his benefactor ; and the little deformed dolls'
dressmaker, with her sot of a father ; and Betty Higden,
the sturdy old woman who has determined neither in life
nor death to suffer the pollution of the workhouse ; such,
with more added, are the ingredients of the story.

One episode, however, deserves longer comment. It
is briefly this : Eugene Wrayburn is a young barrister of
good family and education, and of excellent abilities and
address, all gifts that he has turned to no creditable
purpose whatever.   He falls in with a girl, Lizzie
Hexham, of more than humble rank, but of great beauty
and good character. She interests him, and in mere wanton
carelessness, for he certainly has no idea of offering
marriage, he gains her affection, neither meaning, in any
definite way, to do anything good nor anything bad with
it.   There is another man who loves Lizzie, a schoolmaster, who, in his dull, plodding way, has made the best

of his intellect, and risen in life. He naturally, and we may say properly, for no good can come of them, resents Wrayburn's attentions, as does the girl's brother. Wrayburn uses the superior advantages of his position to insult them in the most offensive and brutal manner, and to torture the schoolmaster, just as he has used those advantages to win the girl's heart. Whereupon, after being goaded to heart's desire for a considerable time, the schoolmaster as nearly as possible beats out Wrayburn's life, and commits suicide. Wrayburn is rescued by Lizzie as he lies by the river bank sweltering in blood, and tended by her, and they are married and live happy ever afterwards.

Now the amazing part of this story is, that Dickens' sympathies throughout are with Wrayburn. How this comes to be so I confess I do not know. To me Wrayburn's conduct appears to be heartless, cruel, unmanly, and the use of his superior social position against the schoolmaster to be like a foul blow, and quite unworthy of a gentleman. Schoolmasters ought not to beat people about the head, decidedly. But if Wrayburn's thoughts took a right course during convalescence, I think he may have reflected that he deserved his beating, and also that the woman whose affection he had won was a great deal too good for him.

Dickens' misplaced sympathy in this particular story has, I repeat, always struck me with amazement. Usually his sympathies are so entirely right. Nothing is more common than to hear the accusation of vulgarity made against his books. A certain class of people seem to think, most mistakenly, that because he so often wrote about vulgar people, uneducated people, people in the lower ranks of society, therefore his writing was vulgar, nay more, he himself vulgar too. Such an opinion can only be based on a strange confusion between subject and treatment. There is scarcely any subject not tainted by impurity, that cannot be treated with entire refinement. Washington Irving wrote to Dickens, most justly, of "that exquisite tact that enabled him to carry his reader through the veriest dens of vice and villainy without a breath to shock the ear or a stain to sully the robe of the most shrinking delicacy;" and added: "It is a rare gift to be able to paint low life without being low, and to be comic without the least taint of vulgarity." This is well said; and if we look for the main secret of the inherent refinement of Dickens' books, we shall find it, I think, in this: that he never intentionally paltered with right and wrong. He would make allowance for evil, would take pleasure in showing that there were streaks of lingering good in its blackness, would treat it kindly, gently, humanly. But it always stood for evil, and nothing else. He made no attempt by cunning jugglery to change its seeming. He had no sneaking affection for it. And therefore, I say again, his attachment to Eugene Wrayburn has always struck me with surprise. As regards Dickens' own refinement, I cannot perhaps do better than quote the words of Sir Arthur Helps, an excellent judge. "He was very refined in his conversation—at least, what I call refined—for he was one of those persons in whose society one is comfortable from the certainty that they will never say anything which can shock other people, or hurt their feelings, be they ever so fastidious or sensitive."

CHAPTER XIII

B UT we are now, alas, nearing the point where the "rapid" of Dickens' life began to "shoot to its fall." The year 1865, during which he partly wrote "Our Mutual Friend," was a fatal one in his career. In the month of February he had been very ill, with an affection of the left foot, at first thought to be merely local, but which really pointed to serious mischief, and never afterwards wholly left him. Then, on June 9th, when returning from France, where he had gone to recruit, he as nearly as possible lost his life in a railway accident at Staplehurst. A bridge had broken in; some of the carriages fell through, and were smashed; that in which Dickens was, hung down the side of the chasm. Of courage and presence of mind he never showed any lack. They were evinced, on one occasion, at the readings, when an alarm of fire arose. They shone conspicuous here. He quieted two ladies who were in the same compartment of the carriage; helped to extricate them and others from their perilous position; gave such help as he could to the wounded and dying; probably was the means of saving the life of one man, whom he was the first to hear faintly groaning under a heap of wreckage; and then, as he tells in the "postcript" to the book, scrambled

back into the carriage to find the crumpled MS. of a portion of "Our Mutual Friend." [1]   But even pluck is power-
less to prevent a ruinous shock to the nerves.   Though
Dickens had done so manfully what he had to do at the
time, he never fully recovered from the blow.   His
daughter tells us how he would often, "when travelling
home from London, suddenly fall into a paroxysm of
fear, tremble all over, clutch the arms of the railway
carriage, large beads of perspiration standing on his face,
and suffer agonies of terror. . . . He had . . . apparently
no idea of our presence."   And Mr. Dolby tells us also
how in travelling it was often necessary for him to ward
off such attacks by taking brandy.   Dickens had been
failing before only too surely ; and this accident, like a
coward's blow, struck him heavily as he fell.

But whether failing or stricken, he bated no jot of
energy or courage ; nay, rather, as his health grew weaker,
did he redouble the pressure of his work.   I think there
is a grandeur in the story of the last five years of his life,
that dwarfs even the tale of his rapid and splendid rise.
It reads like some antique myth of the Titans defying
Jove's thunder.   There is about the man something indomitable and heroic.   He had, as we have seen, given
a series of readings in 1858–59 ; and he gave another in
the years 1861 to 1863—successful enough in a pecuniary
sense, but through failure of business capacity on the part
of the manager, entailing on the reader himself a great
deal of anxiety and worry.[2]   Now, in the spring of 1866,

---

[1] For his own graphic account of the accident, see his "Letters."
[2] He computed that he had made £12,000 by the two first series
of readings.

with his left foot giving him unceasing trouble, and his
nerves shattered, and his heart in an abnormal state, he
accepted an offer from Messrs. Chappell to read "in
England, Ireland, Scotland, and Paris," for £1,500, and
the payment of all expenses, and then to give forty-two
more readings for £2,500. Mr. Dolby, who accompanied
Dickens as business manager in this and the remaining
tours, has told their story in an interesting volume.[1] Of
course the wear was immense. The readings themselves
involved enormous fatigue to one who so identified himself with what he read, and whose whole being seemed
to vibrate not only with the emotions of the characters in
his stories, but of the audience. Then there was the
weariness of long railway journeys in all seasons and
weathers—journeys that at first must have been rendered
doubly tedious, as he could not bear to travel by express
trains. Yet, notwithstanding failure of strength, notwithstanding fatigue, his native gaiety and good spirits
smile like a gleam of winter sunlight over the narrative.
As he had been the brightest and most genial of companions in the old holiday days when strolling about the
country with his actor-troupe, so now he was occasionally
as frolic as a boy, dancing a hornpipe in the train for
the amusement of his companions, compounding bowls
of punch in which he shared but sparingly — for
he was really convivial only in idea—and always
considerate and kindly towards his companions and
dependents. And mingled pathetically with all this are

[1] " Charles Dickens as I Knew Him." By George Dolby. Miss
Dickens considers this " the best and truest picture of her father
yet written."

confessions of pain, weariness, illness, faintness, sleeplessness, internal bleeding,—all bravely borne, and never
for an instant suffered to interfere with any business
arrangement.

But if the strain of the readings was too heavy here at
home, what was it likely to be during a winter in America ?
Nevertheless he determined, against all remonstrances, to
go thither.   It would almost seem as if he felt that the
day of his life was waning, and that it was his duty to
gather in a golden harvest for those he loved ere the
night came on.   So he sailed for Boston once more on
the 9th of November, 1867.   The Americans, it must be
said, behaved nobly.   All the old grudges connected
with "The American Notes," and " Martin Chuzzlewit,"
sank into oblivion.   The reception was everywhere en-
thusiastic, the success of the readings immense.   Again
and again people waited all night, amid the rigours of an
almost arctic winter, in order to secure an opportunity of
purchasing tickets as soon as the ticket office opened.
There were enormous and intelligent audiences at Boston,
New York, Washington, Philadelphia—everywhere.   The
sum which Dickens realized by the tour, amounted to the
splendid total of nearly £19,000.   Nor, in this money
triumph, did he fail to excite his usual charm of personal
fascination, though the public affection and admiration
were manifested in forms less objectionable and offensive
than of old.   On his birthday, the 7th of February, 1868,
he says, " I couldn't help laughing at myself . . .; it
was observed so much as though I were a little boy."
Flowers, garlands were set about his room ; there were
presents on his dinner-table, and in the evening the hall

where he read was decorated by kindly unknown hands. Of public and private entertainment he might have had just as much as he chose.

But to this medal there was a terrible reverse. Travelling from New York to Boston just before Christmas, he took a most disastrous cold, which never left him so long as he remained in the country. He was constantly faint. He ate scarcely anything. He slept very little. Latterly he was so lame, as scarcely to be able to walk. Again and again it seemed impossible that he should fulfil his night's engagement. He was constantly so exhausted at the conclusion of the reading, that he had to lie down for twenty minutes or half an hour, "before he could undergo the fatigue even of dressing." Mr. Dolby lived in daily fear lest he should break down altogether. "I used to steal into his room," he says, "at all hours of the night and early morning, to see if he were awake, or in want of anything; always though to find him wide awake, and as cheerful and jovial as circumstances would admit—never in the least complaining, and only reproaching me for not taking my night's rest." "Only a man of iron will could have accomplished what he did," says Mr. Fields, who knew him well, and saw him often during the tour.

In the first week of May, 1868, Dickens was back in England, and soon again in the thick of his work and play. Mr. Wills, the sub-editor of *All the Year Round*, had met with an accident. Dickens supplied his place. Chauncy Hare Townshend had asked him to edit a chaotic mass of religious lucubrations. He toilfully edited them. Then, with the autumn, the readings

began again ;—for it marks the indomitable energy of the
man that, even amid the terrible physical trials incident
to his tour in America, he had agreed with Messrs.
Chappell, for a sum of £8,000, to give one hundred
more readings after his return. So in October the old
work began again, and he was here, there, and everywhere, now reading at Manchester and Liverpool, now
at Edinburgh and Glasgow, anon coming back to read fitfully in London, then off again to Ireland, or the West of
England. Nor is it necessary to say that he spared himself
not one whit. In order to give novelty to these readings,
which were to be positively the last, he had laboriously
got up the scene of Nancy's murder, in "Oliver Twist,"
and persisted in giving it night after night, though of all his
readings it was the one that exhausted him most terribly.[1]
But of course this could not last. The pain in his foot
"was always recurring at inconvenient and unexpected
moments," says Mr. Dolby, and occasionally the American
cold came back too. In February, in London, the foot
was worse than it had ever been, so bad that Sir Henry
Thompson, and Mr. Beard, his medical adviser, compelled him to postpone a reading. At Edinburgh, a
few days afterwards, Mr. Syme, the eminent surgeon,
strongly recommended perfect rest. Still he battled on,
but "with great personal suffering such as few men could
have endured." Sleeplessness was on him too. And
still he fought on, determined, if it were physically pos-

---

[1] Mr. Dolby remonstrated on this, and it was in connection with a
very slight show of temper on the occasion that he says : "In all
my experiences with the Chief that was the only time I ever heard
him address angry words to any one."

sible, to fulfil his engagement with Messrs. Chappell, and complete the hundred nights. But it was not to be. Symptoms set in that pointed alarmingly towards paralysis of the left side. At Preston, on the 22nd of April, Mr. Beard, who had come post-haste from London, put a stop to the readings, and afterwards decided, in consultation with Sir Thomas Watson, that they ought to be suspended entirely for the time, and never resumed in connection with any railway travelling.

Even this, however, was not quite the end; for a summer of comparative rest, or what Dickens considered rest, seemed so far to have set him up that he gave a final series of twelve readings in London between the 11th of January and 15th of March, 1870, thus bringing to its real conclusion an enterprise by which, at whatever cost to himself, he had made a sum of about £45,000.

Meanwhile, in the autumn of 1869, he had gone back to the old work, and was writing a novel, " The Mystery of Edwin Drood." It is a good novel unquestionably. Without going so far as Longfellow, who had doubts whether it was not "the most beautiful of all" Dickens' works, one may admit that there is about it a singular freshness, and no sign at all of mental decay. As for the " mystery," I do not think *that* need baffle us altogether. But then I see no particular reason to believe that Dickens had wished to baffle us, or specially to rival Edgar Allan Poe or Mr. Wilkie Collins in the construction of criminal puzzles. Even though only half the case is presented to us, and the book remains for ever unfinished, we need have, I think, no difficulty in working out its conclusion. The course pursued by Mr. Jasper,

Lay Precentor of the Cathedral at Cloisterham, is really too suspicious. No intelligent British jury, seeing the facts as they are presented to us, the readers, could for a moment think of acquitting him of the murder of his nephew, Edwin Drood. Take those facts seriatim. First, we have the motive : he is passionately in love with the girl to whom his nephew is engaged. Then we have a terrible coil of compromising circumstances : his extravagant profession of devotion to his nephew, his attempts to establish a hidden influence over the girl's mind to his nephew's detriment and his own advantage, his gropings amid the dark recesses of the Cathedral and inquiries into the action of quicklime, his endeavours to foment a quarrel between Edwin Drood and a fiery young gentleman from Ceylon, on the night of the murder, and his undoubted doctoring of the latter's drink. Then, after the murder, how damaging is his conduct. He falls into a kind of fit on discovering that his nephew's engagement had been broken off, which he might well do if his crime turned out to be not only a crime but also a blunder. And his conduct to the girl is, to say the least of it, strange. Nor will his character help him. He frequents the opium dens of the East-end of London. Guilty, guilty, most certainly guilty. There is nothing to be said in arrest of judgment. Let the judge put on the black cap, and Jasper be devoted to his merited doom.

Such was the story that Dickens was unravelling in the spring and early summer of 1870. And fortune smiled upon it. He had sold the copyright for the large sum of £7,500, and a half share of the profits after a

sale of twenty-five thousand copies, plus £1,000 for the
advance sheets sent to America ; and the sale was more
than answering his expectations. Nor did prosperity look
favourably on the book alone. It also, in one sense,
showered benefits on the author. He was worth, as the
evidence of the Probate Court was to show only too soon,
a sum of over £80,000. He was happy in his children.
He was universally loved, honoured, courted. "Troops
of friends," though, alas ! death had made havoc among
the oldest, were still his. Never had man exhibited less
inclination to pay fawning court to greatness and social
rank. Yet when the Queen expressed a desire to see
him, as she did in March, 1870, he felt not only pride,
but a gentleman's pleasure in acceding to her wish, and
came away charmed from a long chatting interview. But,
while prosperity was smiling thus, the shadows of his
day of life were lengthening, lengthening, and the night
was at hand.

On Wednesday, June 8th, he seemed in excellent
spirits ; worked all the morning in the Châlet [1] as was his
wont, returned to the house for lunch and a cigar, and
then, being anxious to get on with "Edwin Drood,"
went back to his desk once more. The weather was
superb. All round the landscape lay in fullest beauty of
leafage and flower, and the air rang musically with the
song of birds. What were his thoughts that summer day

[1] The Châlet, since sold and removed, stood at the edge of a kind
of "wilderness," which is separated from Gad's Hill Place by
the high road. A tunnel, constructed by Dickens, connects the
"wilderness" and the garden of the house. Close to the road, in
the "wilderness," and fronting the house, are two fine cedars.

as he sat there at his work? Writing many years before, he had asked whether the "subtle liquor of the blood" may not "perceive, by properties within itself," when danger is imminent, and so "run cold and dull"? Did any such monitor within, one wonders, warn him at all that the hand of death was uplifted to strike, and that its shadow lay upon him? Judging from the words that fell from his pen that day we might almost think that it was so —we might almost go further, and guess with what hopes and fears he looked into the darkness beyond. Never at any time does he appear to have been greatly troubled by speculative doubt. There is no evidence in his life, no evidence in his letters, no evidence in his books, that he had ever seen any cause to question the truth of the reply which Christianity gives to the world-old problems of man's origin and destiny. For abstract speculation he had not the slightest turn or taste. In no single one of his characters does he exhibit any fierce mental struggle as between truth and error. All that side of human experience, with its anguish of battle, its despairs, and its triumphs, seems to have been unknown to him. Perhaps he had the stronger grasp of other matters in consequence—who knows? But the fact remains. With a trust quite simple and untroubled, he held through life to the faith of Christ. When his children were little, he had written prayers for them, had put the Bible into simpler language for their use. In his will, dated May 12, 1869, he had said, " I commit my soul to the mercy of God through our Lord and Saviour Jesus Christ, and I exhort my dear children humbly to try to guide themselves by the broad teaching of the New Testament in its broad spirit, and to put no faith in any man's narrow construction of its letter here or there." And now, on this last day of his life, in probably the last letter that left his pen, he wrote to one who had objected to some passage in "Edwin Drood" as irreverent : "I have always striven in my writings to express veneration for the life and lessons of our Saviour—because I feel it." And with a significance, of which, as I have said, he may himself have been dimly half-conscious, among the last words of his unfinished story, written that very afternoon, are words that tell of glorious summer sunshine trans-figuring the city of his imagination, and of the changing lights, and the song of birds, and the incense from garden and meadow that "penetrate into the cathedral" of Cloisterham, "subdue its earthy odour, and preach the Resurrection and the Life."

For now the end had come. When he went in to dinner Miss Hogarth noticed that he looked very ill, and wished at once to send for a doctor. But he refused, struggled for a short space against the impending fit, and tried to talk, at last very incoherently. Then, when urged to go up to his bed, he rose, and, almost imme-diately, slid from her supporting arm, and fell on the floor. Nor did consciousness return. He passed from the unrest of life into the peace of eternity on the follow-ing day, June 9, 1870, at ten minutes past six in the evening.

And now he lies in Westminster Abbey, among the men who have most helped, by deed or thought, to make this England of ours what it is. Dean Stanley only gave effect to the national voice when he assigned to him that place of sepulture. The most popular, and in most respects the greatest novelist of his time ; the lord over the laughter and tears of a whole generation ; the writer, in his own field of fiction, whose like we shall probably not see again for many a long, long year, if ever ; where could he be laid more fittingly for his last long sleep than in the hallowed resting-place which the country sets apart for the most honoured of her children ?

So he lies there among his peers in the Southern Transept. Close beside him sleep Dr. Johnson, the puissant literary autocrat of his own time ; and Garrick, who was that time's greatest actor ; and Handel, who may fittingly claim to have been one of the mightiest musicians of all time. There sleeps, too, after the fitful fever of his troubled life, the witty, the eloquent Sheridan. In close proximity rests Macaulay, the artist-historian and essayist. Within the radius of a few yards lies all that will ever die of Chaucer, who five hundred years ago sounded the spring note of English literature, and gave to all after-time the best, brightest glimpse into mediæval England ; and all that is mortal also of Spenser of the honey'd verse ; and of Beaumont, who had caught an echo of Shakespeare's sweetness if not his power ; and of sturdy Ben Jonson, held in his own day a not unworthy rival of Shakespeare's self ; and of " glorious " and most masculine John Dryden. From his monument Shakespeare looks upon the place with his kindly eyes, and Addison too, and Goldsmith ; and one can almost imagine a smile of fellowship upon the marble faces of those later dead—Burns, Coleridge, Southey, and Thackeray.

Nor in that great place of the dead does Dickens enjoy cold barren honour alone. Nearly seventeen years have gone by since he was laid there—yes, nearly seventeen years, though it seems only yesterday that I was listening to the funeral sermon in which Dean Stanley spoke of the simple and sufficient faith in which he had lived and died. But though seventeen years have gone by, yet are outward signs not wanting of the peculiar love that clings to him still. As I strolled through the Abbey this last Christmas Eve I found his grave, and his grave alone, made gay with the season's hollies. " Lord, keep my memory green,"—in another sense than he used the words, that prayer is answered.

And of the future what shall we say ? His fame had a brilliant day while he lived; it has a brilliant day now. Will it fade into twilight, without even an after-glow ; will it pass altogether into the night of oblivion ? I cannot think so. The vitality of Dickens' works is singularly great. They are all a-throb, as it were, with hot human blood. They are popular in the highest sense because their appeal is universal, to the uneducated as well as the educated. The humour is superb, and most of it, so far as one can judge, of no ephemeral kind. The pathos is more questionable, but that too, at its simplest and best, and especially when the humour is shot with it—is worthy of a better epithet than excellent. It is supremely touching. Imagination, fancy, wit, elo-quence, the keenest observation, the most strenuous en-deavour to reach the highest artistic excellence, the largest kindliness,—all these he brought to his life-work. And that work, as I think, will live, I had almost dared to prophesy for ever.   Of course fashions change.   Of course no writer of fiction, writing for his own little day, can per-manently meet the needs of all after times.   Some loss of immediate vital interest is inevitable.   Nevertheless, in Dickens' case, all will not die.   Half a century, a century hence, he will still be read; not perhaps as he was read when his words flashed upon the world in their first glory and freshness, nor as he is read now in the noon of his fame. But he will be read much more than we read the novelists of the last century—be read as much, shall I say, as we still read Scott.   And so long as he *is* read, there will be one gentle and humanizing influence the more at work among men.

THE END.

INDEX.

BIBLIOGRAPHY.

BY

JOHN P. ANDERSON

(British Museum).

I. Works.

II. Selections.

III. Single Works.

IV. Miscellaneous Works.

V. Appendix—
Biographical, Critical, etc.
Dramatic.
Musical.
Parodies and Imitations.
Poetical.
Magazine and Newspaper Articles.

VI. Chronological List of Works.

I. WORKS.

First Cheap Edition. 19 vols. London, 1847-67, 8vo.
This edition was in three series, the first and third being published by Messrs. Chapman and Hall, the second by Messrs. Bradbury and Evans. It was printed in double columns, with frontispieces by Leslie, Hablôt K. Browne, Cruikshank, etc.

Library Edition. 22 vols. London, 1858-59, 8vo.

Library Edition. Illustrated. 30 vols. London, 1861-1873.
The original illustrations were added to the later issues of the Library Edition, and the series completed in 30 vols.

The People's Edition. 25 vols. London, 1865-1867, 8vo.
A re-issue of the Cheap Edition.

The Charles Dickens Edition. Illustrated. 21 vols. London, 1867-1873, 8vo.

The Household Edition. Illustrated. 22 vols. London, 1871-1879, 4to.

Illustrated Library Edition. 30 vols. London, 1873-1876, 8vo.

The Popular Library Edition. Illustrated. 30 vols. London, 1878-1880, 8vo.

The Pocket Edition. 30 vols. London, 1880, 16mo.

The Diamond Edition. Illustrated. 14 vols. London, 1880, 16mo.

Édition de Luxe. Illustrated. 30 vols. London, 1881, 4to.
, One thousand copies only of this Édition de Luxe were printed for sale, each numbered, and it was dedicated to Her Majesty the Queen.

The Cabinet Edition. Illustrated. London, 1885, etc., 16mo.
A re-issue of the Pocket Edition.

II. SELECTIONS.

The Beauties of Pickwick. Collected and arranged by Sam Weller. London, 1838, 8vo.

The Story Teller. A collection of tales, stories, and novels. By Walter Scott, Washington Irving, Charles Dickens, etc. Edited by Hermann Schütz. Siegen, 1850, 8vo.

Immortelles from C. D. By Ich. London, 1856, 8vo.

Novels and Tales reprinted from Household Words. 11 vols. (*Tauchnitz Edition*). Leipzig, 1856-59, 16mo.

Christmas Stories from the Household Words. Conducted by C. D. London [1860], 8vo.

The Poor Traveller : Boots at the Holly-Tree Inn ; and Mrs. Gamp, by C. D. London, 1858, 8vo.
    Arranged by Dickens for his Readings.

Dialogues from Dickens. Arranged by W. E. Fette. Two Series. Boston, 1870-71, 8vo.

A Cyclopædia of the best thoughts of C. D. Compiled and alphabetically arranged by F. G. De Fontaine. New York, 1873, 8vo.

A Series of Character Sketches from Dickens. Being fac-similes of original drawings by F. Barnard [with extracts from some of D.'s works]. 2 pts. London [1879]-85, folio.

——Another Edition. London, 1884, folio.

The Dickens Reader. Character Readings from the stories of Charles Dickens. Selected, adapted, and arranged by Nathan Sheppard, with numerous illustrations by F. Barnard, New York, 1881, 4to.

The Charles Dickens Birthday Book. Compiled and edited by his eldest daughter (Mary Dickens). With illustrations by his youngest daughter (Kate Perugini). London, 1882, 8vo.

Readings from the works of C. D. Condensed and adapted by J. A. Jennings. Dublin [1882], 8vo.

The Readings of C. D. as arranged and read by himself. With illustrations. London, 1883, 8vo.

Chips from Dickens selected by Thomas Mason. Glasgow [1884], 32mo.

Tales from Charles Dickens's Works. London [1884], 8vo.

The Humour and Pathos of Charles Dickens. Selected by Chas. Kent. London, 1884, 8vo.

Child-Pictures from Dickens. [Illustrated.] London, 1885, 4to

Wellerisms from "Pickwick" and "Master Humphrey's Clock." Selected by Charles F. Rideal, and Edited, with an Introduction, by Charles Kent, author of "The Humour and Pathos of Charles Dickens." London, 1886, 8vo.

III. SINGLE WORKS.

American Notes for general circulation. 2 vols. London, 1842, 8vo.

——[Other Editions. London, 1850, 8vo.; London, 1884, 8vo].

Bleak House. With illustrations, by H. K. Browne. London, 1853, 8vo.

Boots at the Holly-Tree Inn, by Charles Dickens, as condensed by himself for his readings. Boston, 1868, 8vo.

The Holly-Tree Inn was the Christmas Number of "Household Words" for 1855. Dickens contributed "The Guest," "The Boots," and "The Bill."

A Child's History of England. With a frontispiece by F. W. Topham. 3 vols. London, 1852-54, 16mo.

The Chimes: a Goblin Story of some bells that rang an old year out and a new year in. By Charles Dickens. [Illustrated by Maclise, Doyle, Leech, and Clarkson Stanfield.] London, 1845, 8vo.

An edition with notes and elucidations by K. ten Bruggencate was published at Groningen in 1883.

Christmas Books. London, 1852, 8vo.

Christmas Books. With illustrations by Sir E. Landseer, Maclise, Stanfield, F. Stone, Doyle, Leech, and Tenniel. London, 1869, 8vo.

A Christmas Carol in Prose. Being a Ghost Story of Christmas. By C. D. With illustrations by John Leech. London, 1843, 8vo.

——Condensed by himself, for his readings. Boston [U.S.], 1868, 8vo.

The Cricket on the Hearth. A Fairy Tale of Home. By C. D. [Illustrated by Maclise, Doyle, Clarkson Stanfield, Leech, and Landseer.] London, 1846, 16mo.

The Battle of Life : A Love Story. [Illustrated by Maclise, Stanfield, Doyle, and Leech.] London, 1846, 16mo.

The Haunted Man and the Ghost's Bargain. A Fancy for Christmas Time. [Illustrated by Stanfield, John Tenniel, Frank Stone, and John Leech.] London, 1848, 16mo.

Dealings with the Firm of Dombey and Son, wholesale, retail, and for exportation. With illustrations by H. K. Browne. London, 1848, 8vo.

The Story of Little Dombey. By C. D. London, 1858, 8vo.

Revised by Dickens for his Readings.

The Story of Little Dombey. By C. D., as condensed by himself for his readings. Boston [U.S.], 1868, 8vo.

Doctor Marigold's Prescriptions. (*Tauchnitz Edition*, vol. 894.) Leipzig, 1867, 16mo.

The Christmas Number of "All the Year Round" for 1865. Dickens contributed chap. i., " To be Taken Immediately ;" chap. vi., "To be Taken With a Grain of Salt ; " and the concluding chapter, "To be Taken for Life."

Doctor Marigold. By C. D., as condensed by himself for his readings. Boston [U.S.], 1868, 8vo.

Great Expectations. By C. D. In three volumes. London, 1861, 8vo.

Appeared originally in *All the Year Round*, December 1, 1860, to August 3, 1861. An American edition was published the same year with illustrations by J. McLenan.

Hard Times. For these Times. By C. D. London, 1854, 8vo.

Appeared originally in Household Words, April 1 to August 12, 1854.

Hunted Down. (*Tauchnitz Edition*, vol. 536.) Leipzig, 1860, 16mo.

Appeared originally in the *New York Ledger*, August 20, 27, Sept. 3, 1859, and *All the Year Round*, Aug. 4 and 11, 1860.

Hunted Down. A Story. By C. D. With some account of T. G. Wainewright, the poisoner [by John Camden Hotten]. London [1870], 8vo.

Is She his Wife? or, Something Singular. A comic burletta in one act. Boston [U.S.], 1877, 16mo.
First produced at the St. James's Theatre, March 6, 1837. Mr. Shepherd says that this was first printed in 1837, but no copy is know to exist.

The Lamplighter: A Farce. By C. D. (1838).
Only 250 copies were privately printed in 1879 from the MS. copy in the Forster Collection at South Kensington; each copy numbered.

The Life and Adventures of Martin Chuzzlewit. With illustrations by Phiz [*i.e.*, H. K. Browne]. London, 1844, 8vo.

Mrs. Gamp [extracted from "The Life and Adventures of Martin Chuzzlewit"]. By C. D., as condensed by himself, for his readings. Boston [U.S.], 1868, 8vo.

The Life and Adventures of Nicholas Nickleby. With illustrations by Phiz. London, 1839, 8vo.
Contains a portrait of Dickens, and 39 illustrations.

Nicholas Nickleby at the Yorkshire School [extracted from "The Life and Adventures of Nicholas Nickleby"]. By C. D., as condensed by himself, for his readings. (Four Chapters). Boston [U.S.], 1868, 8vo.
Another edition in three chapters was published at Boston the same year.

Little Dorrit. With illustrations, by H. K. Browne. London [1855]-57, 8vo.

Master Humphrey's Clock. With illustrations by George Cattermole and H. K. Browne. 3 vols. London, 1840-41, 8vo.
Comprises two stories, "The Old Curiosity Shop" and "Barnaby Rudge," both subsequently issued as independent works, the first in 1848, and the second in 1849.

The Old Curiosity Shop. London, 1848, 8vo.

Barnaby Rudge. A Tale of the Riots of Eighty. London, 1849, 8vo.

Mr. Nightingale's Diary: a Farce, in one act. London, 1851, 8vo.
Privately printed and extremely scarce. There is a copy in the Forster Collection at South Kensington.
——Another edition. Boston [U.S.], 1877, 16mo.
This edition is now scarce.

The Mudfog Papers. Now first collected. London, 1880, 8vo.
Reprinted from Bentley's Miscellany.
——Second edition. London, 1880, 8vo.

The Mystery of Edwin Drood. With twelve illustrations by S. L. Fildes, and a portrait. London, 1870, 8vo.

Oliver Twist; or, The Parish Boy's Progress. By "Boz." In three volumes. [With illustrations by George Cruikshank.] London, 1838, 8vo.
The second edition, with the title-page reading "Oliver Twist, by Charles Dickens," appeared the following year; the third edition, with a new preface, was published in 1841. The edition of 1846, in one volume, bears the following title-page:—"The Adventures of Oliver Twist; or, The Parish Boy's Progress. By Charles Dickens. With twenty-four illustrations on Steel, by George Cruikshank."

Our Mutual Friend. With illus-

trations by Marcus Stone. 2 vols. London, 1865, 8vo.
The Personal History of David Copperfield. With illustrations, by H. K. Browne. London, 1850, 8vo.
David Copperfield. By C. D., as condensed by himself, for his readings. Boston [U.S.], 1868, 8vo.
Pictures from Italy. By C. D. The vignette illustrations on wood, by Samuel Palmer. London, 1846, 8vo.
Appeared originally in the *Daily News*, from January to March 1846, with the title of "Travelling Letters written on the Road. By Charles Dickens."
The Posthumous Papers of the Pickwick Club. Being a faithful record of the Perambulations, Perils, Travels, Adventures, and Sporting Transactions of the Corresponding Members. Edited by "Boz." With forty-three illustrations by R. Seymour, R. W. Buss, and Phiz [H. K. Browne]. London, 1837, 8vo.
In twenty monthly parts, commencing April 1836, and ending November 1837, no number being issued for June 1837.
——Another edition. V. D. Land, Launceston, 1838, 8vo.
This edition of Pickwick is interesting from the fact that it was published in Van Dieman's Land, the illustrations being exact copies of the originals executed in lithography. There is an additional title-page, engraved, bearing date 1836.
——The Posthumous Papers of the Pickwick Club, with notes and illustrations. Edited by C. Dickens the younger. (Jubilee Edition.) 2 vols. London, 1886, 8vo.
Mr. Bob. Sawyer's Party [extracted from "The Posthumous Papers of the Pickwick Club"] by

C. D., as condensed by himself, for his readings. Boston [U.S.], 1868, 8vo.
Bardell and Pickwick [extracted from "The Posthumous Papers of the Pickwick Club"] by C. D., as condensed by himself, for his readings. Boston [U.S.], 1868, 8vo.
Sketches by "Boz," illustrative of every-day life and every-day people. In two volumes. Illustrations by George Cruikshank. London, 1836, 12mo.
——Second edition. London, 1836, 12mo.
Sketches by "Boz." Third edition. London, 1837, 12mo.
——Second Series. London, 1837, 12mo.
——First complete edition of the two series. With forty illustrations by George Cruikshank. London, 1839, 8vo.
——Sketches and Tales of London Life. [Selections from "Sketches by Boz."] London [1877], 8vo.
——The Tuggs's at Ramsgate [from "Sketches by Boz"]. London [1870], 8vo.
Sketches of Young Gentlemen. Dedicated to the Young Ladies. With six illustrations by "Phiz" (H. K. Browne). London, 1838, 8vo.
Sketches of Young Couples; with an urgent Remonstrance to the Gentlemen of England (being Bachelors or Widowers) on the present alarming Crisis. With six illustrations by "Phiz" [H. K. Browne]. London, 1840, 8vo.
An edition was published in 1869 with the title "Sketches of Young Couples, Young Ladies, Young Gentlemen. By Quiz. Illustrated

by Phiz." Only the first and third of these sketches were written by Charles Dickens. "The Sketches of Young Ladies" were by an anonymous author, who also assumed the pseudonym of Quiz.

Somebody's Luggage. (*Tauchnitz Edition*, vol. 888.) Leipzig, 1867, 16mo.
  The Christmas Number of *All the Year Round* for 1862. Dickens contributed "His leaving it till called for"; "His Boots"; "His Brown-paper Parcel" and "His Wonderful End."

The Strange Gentleman : A Comic Burletta. In two acts. By "Boz." First performed at the St. James's Theatre, on Thursday, September 29, 1836. London, 1837, 8vo.

Sunday under Three Heads. As it is ; as Sabbath bills would make it ; as it might be made. By Timothy Sparks. London, 1836, 12mo.
  Reproduced in fac-simile, London, 1884, and in Pearson's Manchester Series of Fac-simile Reprints, Manchester, same date.

A Tale of Two Cities. With illustrations by H. K. Browne. London, 1859, 8vo.
  Originally issued in *All the Year Round*, between April 30 and November 26, 1859.

The Uncommercial Traveller. By C. D. London, 1861, 8vo.
  Consists of seventeen papers which originally appeared in *All the Year Round* with this title between January 28 and October 13, 1860. The impression which was issued in 1868 in the Charles Dickens Edition contains eleven fresh papers.

The Village Coquettes : A Comic Opera. In two acts. By C. D. The music by John Hullah. London, 1836, 8vo.
—— Songs, choruses, and concerted pieces in the Operatic Burletta of The Village Coquet-

tes as produced at St. James's Theatre. The drama and words of the songs by "Boz." The music by John Hullah. London, 1837, 8vo.
  Editions of "The Village Coquettes" were published at Leipzig, 1845, and at Amsterdam, 1868, in English, and it was reprinted in 1878. *See* also under *Music.*

IV.

MISCELLANEOUS WORKS.

All the Year Round. A weekly journal conducted by Charles Dickens. London, 1859-1870, 8vo.
  Commenced on the 30th of April 1859.

Bentley's Miscellany. [Successively edited by Boz, Ainsworth, Albert Smith, etc.] Vol. 1-64. London, 1837-68, 8vo.

Evenings of a Working Man, being the occupation of his scanty leisure. By John Overs. With a preface relative to the author, by C. D. London, 1844, 16mo.

Household Words : a weekly journal. Conducted by C. D. 19 vols. London, 1850-59, 8vo.
  This Journal commenced on the 30th March 1850, and was continued to the 28th of May 1859, when it was incorporated with *All the Year Round.* A cheap edition of Household Words, in 19 vols. was published in 1868-73.

—— Christmas Stories from Household Words (1850-58). Conducted by C. D. London, [1860], 8vo.

Legends and Lyrics, by Adelaide Anne Procter. With an introduction by C. D. New edition, illustrated by Dobson, Palmer, Tenniel, etc. London, 1866, 4to.

The Letters of C. D. Edited by his sister-in-law (G. Hogarth) and his eldest daughter (M. Dickens). 3 vols. London, 1880-1882, 8vo.
——Another edition. 2 vols. London, 1882, 8vo.
The Library of Fiction ; or Family Story-Teller. [Edited by C. D.] London, 1836-37, 8vo.
The Loving Ballad of Lord Bateman. Illustrated by George Cruikshank. London, 1839, 8vo.
The notes and preface were written by Dickens.
Memoirs of Joseph Grimaldi. Edited by " Boz." With illustrations by G. Cruikshank. 2 vols. London, 1838, 12mo.
Memoirs of Joseph Grimaldi. Another edition. Revised by C. Whitehead. London, 1846, 8vo.
——Another edition. London, 1853, 8vo.
——Another edition. London, 1866, 8vo.
Two other editions were published in 1884 by G. Routledge and Sons, and J. Dicks.
The Newsvendors' Benevolent and Provident Institution. Speeches on behalf of the Institution by C. D. London, 1871, 8vo.
The Pic-Nic Papers by various hands. Edited by C. D. With illustrations by George Cruikshank. 3 vols. London, 1841, 8vo.
Dickens contributed a preface and the opening tale, "' The Lamp-lighter's Story."
The Plays and Poems of Charles Dickens. With a few Miscellanies in prose. Now first collected, edited, prefaced, and and annotated by R. H.

Shepherd. 2 vols. London, 1882, 8vo.
This work was almost immediately suppressed, as it contained copyright matter. A new edition appeared in 1885, without the copyright play of " No Thoroughfare."
Religious Opinions of Chauncy Hare Townshend. Published as directed in his Will, by his literary executor [Charles Dickens]. London, 1869, 8vo.
Royal Literary Fund. A summary of facts in answer to allegations contained in " The Case of the Reformers of the Literary Fund," stated by C. D., etc. [London, 1858], 8vo.
Speech delivered at the meeting of the Administrative Reform Association. London, 1855, 8vo.
Speech of C. D. as Chairman of the Anniversary Festival Dinner of the Royal Free Hospital, 1863. [London, 1870], 12mo.
The Speeches of C. D., 1841-1870, edited and prefaced by R. H. Shepherd. With a new bibliography, revised and enlarged. London, 1884, 8vo.
Speeches, letters, and sayings of C. D. To which is added a Sketch of the author by G. A. Sala, and Dean Stanley's sermon. New York, 1870, 8vo.
Speeches : Literary and Social. London [1870], 8vo.
A Wonderful Ghost Story. With l.tters of C. D. to the author respecting it. By Thomas Heaphy. London, 1882, 8vo.

V. APPENDIX.

BIOGRAPHICAL, CRITICAL, ETC.

Adshead, Joseph. — Prisons and Prisoners. London, 1845, 8vo.

The Fictions of Dickens upon solitary confinement, pp. 95-121.

Allbut, Robert.—London Rambles "En Zigzag," with Charles Dickens. London [1886], 8vo.

Atlantic Almanac.—The Atlantic Almanac for 1871. Boston, 1871, 8vo.
A short biographical notice of Dickens, with portrait and view of Gad's Hill, pp. 20-21.

Bagehot, Walter.—Literary Studies, by the late Walter Bagehot. 2 vols. London, 1879, 8vo.
Charles Dickens (1858), vol. 2, pp. 184-220.

Bayne, Peter.—Essays in Biography and Criticism. By Peter Bayne. First series. Boston, 1857, 8vo.
The modern novel: Dickens, Bulwer, Thackeray, pp. 363-392.

Behn-Eschenburg, H. — Charles Dickens. Von H. Behn-Eschenburg. Basel, 1872, 8vo.
Hft. 6, of "Oeffentliche Vorträge gehalten in der Schweiz."

Brimley, George.—Essays by the late George Brimley. Edited by William George Clark. Cambridge, 1858, 8vo.
"Bleak House," pp. 289 301. Reprinted from the *Spectator*, September 24th, 1853.

Browne, Hablôt K.—Dombey and Son. The four portraits of Edith, Florence, Alice, and Little Paul. London, 1848, 8vo.

——Dombey and Son. Full-length portraits of Dombey and Carker, Miss Tox, Mrs. Skewton, etc. London, 1848, 8vo.

——Six illustrations to The Posthumous Papers of the Pickwick Club. Engraved from original drawings by Phiz. London [1854], 8vo.

Buchanan, Robert. — A Poet's Sketch-Book; selections from the prose writings of Robert Buchanan. London, 1883, 8vo.
The Good Genie of Fiction. Charles Dickens, pp. 119-140. (Reprinted from *St. Paul's Magazine*, 1872, pp. 130-148.)

Calverley, C. S. — Fly Leaves. Second Edition. By C. S. Calverley. Cambridge, 1872, 8vo.
An Examination Paper. "The Posthumous Papers of the Pickwick Club," pp. 121-124.

Canning, S. G.—Philosophy of Charles Dickens. By the Hon. Albert S. G. Canning. London, 1880, 8vo.

Cary, Thomas G.—Letter to a lady in France on the supposed failure of a national bank . . . with answers to enquiries concerning the books of Captain Marryat and Mr. Dickens. [By Thomas G. Cary.] Boston [U.S.], 1843, 8vo.

——Second Edition. Boston, [U.S.], 1844, 8vo.

Chambers, Robert.—Cyclopædia of English Literature. Edited by Robert Chambers. 2 vols. Edinburgh, 1844, 8vo.
Charles Dickens, vol. ii., pp. 630-633.

——Another Edition. 2 vols. Edinburgh, 1860, 8vo.
Charles Dickens, with a portrait, vol. ii., pp. 644-650.

——Third Edition, 2 vols. London, 1876, 8vo.
Charles Dickens, with a portrait, vol. ii., pp. 515-521.

Chapman, T. J.—Schools and Schoolmasters; from the works of Charles Dickens. New York, 1871, 8vo.

Clarke, Charles and Mary Cowden.—Recollections of Writers. By Charles and Mary Cowden Clarke. With letters of Charles Lamb . . . and Charles Dickens, etc. London, 1878, 8vo.

Cleveland, Charles Dexter.—English Literature of the Nineteenth Century. A new edition. Philadelphia, 1867, 8vo.
Charles Dickens, pp. 718-730.

Cochrane, Robert.—Risen by Perseverance ; or, lives of self-made men. By Robert Cochrane. Edinburgh, 1879, 8vo.
Charles Dickens, pp. 172-223.

Cook, James.—Bibliography of the writings of Charles Dickens, with many curious and interesting particulars relating to his works. By James Cook. London, 1879, 8vo.

Cruikshank, George. — George Cruikshank's Magazine. London, 1854, 8vo.
February 1854, pp. 74-80, "A letter from Hop-o'-My-Thumb to Charles Dickens, Esq., upon 'Frauds on the Fairies,' 'Whole Hogs,' etc."

D., H. W.—Ward and Lock's Penny Books for the People. Biographical series. The Life of Charles Dickens. By H. W. D. Pp. 513 - 528. London, 1882, 8vo.

Davey, Samuel.—Darwin, Carlyle and Dickens, with other essays. By Samuel Davey. London, [1876], 8vo.

Denman, Lord. — Uncle Tom's Cabin, Bleak House, Slavery and Slave Trade. Six articles by Lord Denman. London, 1853, 8vo.

——Second Edition. London, 1853, 8vo.

Dépret, Louis.—Chez les Anglais. Shakespeare, Charles Dickens, Longfellow, etc. Paris, 1879, Charles Dickens, 1812-1870, occupies pp. 71-130.

Dickens, Charles.—Chas. Dickens. A critical biography. London, 1858, 8vo.

No. 1 of a series entitled " Our Contemporaries," etc.

——The Life and Times of Charles Dickens. With a portrait. (*Police News* edition.) London. [1870], 8vo.

——The Life of Charles Dickens. London [1881], 8vo.

——The Life of Charles Dickens. London [1882], 8vo.
Part of Haughton's Popular Illustrated Biographies.

——Some Notes on America to be re-written, suggested with respect to Charles Dickens. Philadelphia, 1868, 8vo.

——Catalogue of the beautiful collection of modern pictures, etc., of Charles Dickens, which will be sold by auction by Messrs. Christie, Manson and Woods . . . July 9, 1870. London [1870], 4to.

——Dickens Memento, with introduction by F. Phillimore, and " Hints to Dickens Collectors," by J. F. Dexter. Catalogue with purchasers' names, etc. London [1884], 4to.

——Mary.—Charles Dickens. By his eldest daughter (Mary Dickens). London, 1885, 8vo.
Part of the series " The World's Workers," etc.

Dilke, Charles W.—The Papers of a Critic, etc. 2 vols. London, 1875, 8vo.
Reference to the Literary Fund Controversy, with a letter from C. D. to C. W. Dilke. Vol. i., pp. 79, 80.

Dolby, George.—Charles Dickens as I knew him. The story of the Reading Tours in Great Britain and America (1866-1870). By George Dolby. London, 1885, 8vo.

Drake, Samuel Adams. — Our Great Benefactors ; short biographies, etc. Boston, 1884, 8vo.

Charles Dickens, pp. 102-111, illustrated.

Dulcken, A.—Scenes from "The Pickwick Papers," designed by A Dulcken. London [1861], obl. fol.

——H. W. — Worthies of the World, a series of historical and critical sketches, etc. Edited by H. W. Dulcken. London [1881], 8vo.

Biography of Charles Dickens, with a portrait, pp. 513-528.

Essays.—English Essays. 4 vols. Hamburg, 1870, 8vo.

Vol. iv. contains an article reprinted from the *Illustrated London News*, June 18, 1870, on Charles Dickens.

Field, Kate.—Pen Photographs of Charles Dickens's Readings. Taken from life. By Kate Field. Boston, [U.S.], [1868], 8vo.

——Another edition. Illustrated. Boston (U.S.), 1871, 8vo.

Fields, James T.—In and out of doors with Charles Dickens. By James T. Fields. Boston, (U.S.), 1876, 16mo.

——James T. Fields. Biographical Notes and Personal Sketches. Boston [U.S.], 1881, 8vo.

Pp. 152-160 relate to Dickens.

Fitzgerald, Percy.—Two English Essayists. C. Lamb and C. Dickens. By Percy Fitzgerald. London, 1864, 8vo.

Afternoon Lectures on Literature and Art, series 2.

——R:creations of a Literary Man. By Percy Fitzgerald. 2 vols. London, 1882, 8vo.

Charles Dickens as an editor, vol. i., pp. 48-96 ; Charles Dickens at Home, vol. i., pp. 97-171.

Forster, John. — The Life of Charles Dickens. (With por-

traits.) 3 1872-4, 8vo.

Numerous e(

Friswell, J. H of Letters By J. Hain l 1870, 8vo.

Charles Dic

Frost, Thoma; Charles Dicl

Frost. Lon(Gill. T.—Repc given to (Reported by English. B(8vo.

Hall, Samuel (Memories ol Women of 1 S. C. Hall.

Charles Dic

——Second e 1877, 4to.

Charles Dicl

Ham, James Pa Fiction : a 1 on C. Dicl Panton Harr 8vo

Hanaford, P. A ings of C. York, 1882,

Hassard, John F ian Pilgrimag London of (By John R. ((U S.), 1881, Heavisides, Ed Poetical and Edward M London, 185(The Essay o pp 1-27.

Hollingshead, Essays and M London, 186! Mr. Dickens ii., pp. 277-283 Reader, vol. ii.,

Hollingshead, John. — Miscellanies. Stories and Essays by John Hollingshead. 3 vols. London, 1874, 8vo.
  Mr. Dickens and his critics, voL iii., pp. 270-274; Mr. Dickens as a Reader, vol. iii., pp. 275-283.

Horne, Richard H.—A New Spirit of the Age. Edited by R. H. Horne. 2 vols. London, 1844, 12mo.
  Charles Dickens, with portrait, voL i., pp. 1-76.

Hotten, John Camden.—Charles Dickens, the Story of his Life. By the Author of the Life of Thackeray (J. C. Hotten). With illustrations and facsimiles. London (1870), 8vo.
——Popular edition. London (1873), 12mo.

Hume, A. B. — A Christmas Memorial of Charles Dickens. By A. B. Hume. 1870, 8vo.
  Contains a fac-simile of Charles Dickens's letter to Mr. J. W. Makeham, dated June 8, 1870, and an Ode to his memory.

Hutton, Laurence. — Literary Landmarks of London. By Laurence Hutton. London [1885], 8vo.
  Charles Dickens, 1812-1870, pp. 79-86.

Irving, Walter.—Charles Dickens. [An essay.] By Walter Irving. Edinburgh, 1874, 8vo.

Jeaffreson, J. Cordy.—Novels and Novelists from Elizabeth to Victoria. By J. Cordy Jeaffreson. 2 vols. London, 1858, 8vo.
  Charles Dickens, vol. ii., pp. 303-334.

Jerrold, Blanchard.—The Best of All Good Company. Edited by Blanchard Jerrold. Pt. 1., A Day with Charles Dickens. London, 1871, 8vo.
  Reprinted in 1872, 8vo.

Johnson, Charles Plumptre. — Hints to Collectors of original

editions of the works of Charles Dickens. By Charles Plumptre Johnson. London, 1885, 8vo.

Johnson, Joseph.—Clever Boys of our Time, and how they became famous men. Edinburgh [1878], 8vo.
  Charles Dickens, pp. 40-63.

Jones, Charles H. — Appleton's New Handy-volume Series. A short life of Charles Dickens, etc. By Charles H. Jones. New York, 1880, 8vo.

Joubert, André.—André Joubert. Charles Dickens, sa vie et ses œuvres. Paris, 1872, 8vo.

Kent, Charles. — The Charles Dickens Dinner. An authentic record of the public banquet given to Mr Charles Dickens . . . prior to his departure for the United States. [With a preface signed C. K. *i.e.*, Charles Kent.] London, 1867, 8vo.

Kent, Charles.—Charles Dickens as a Reader. By Charles Kent. London, 1872, 8vo.

Kitton, Fred. G. — "Phiz" (Hablôt Knight Browne.) A Memoir. Including a selection from his Correspondence and Notes on his principal works. By Fred. G. Kitton. With a portrait and numerous illustrations. London, 1882, 8vo.
  An account is given of the relationship that existed between Dickens and Phiz.
——Dickensiana. A Bibliography of the literature relating to Charles Dickens and his writings. Compiled by Fred. G. Langton. London, 1880, 8vo.

Langton, Robert. — Charles Dickens and Rochester, etc. By Robert Kitton. London, 1886, 8vo.

Langton, Robert.—The Childhood and Youth of Charles Dickens, etc. By Robert Langton. Manchester, 1883, 8vo.

L'Estrange, A. G.—History of English Humour, etc. By the Rev. A. G. L'Estrange. 2 vols. London, 1878, 8vo.
Chapter 18 of vol. ii. is devoted to Dickens.

Lynch, Judge.—Judge Lynch (of America), his two letters to Charles Dickens (of England) upon the subject of the Court of Chancery. London, 1859, 8vo.

McCarthy, Justin.—A History of Our Own Times. A new edition. 4 vols. London, 1882, 8vo.
Dickens and Thackeray, vol. ii., pp. 255-259.

McKenzie, Charles H.—The Religious Sentiments of C. D., collected from his writings. By Charles H. McKenzie. Newcastle, 1884, 8vo.

Mackenzie, R. Shelton. — Life of Charles Dickens, etc. By R. Shelton Mackenzie. Philadelphia [1870], 8vo.

Macrae, David. — Home and Abroad; Sketches and Gleanings. By David Macrae. Glasgow, 1871, 8vo.
Carlyle and Dickens, pp. 122-128.

Masson, David.—British Novelists and their styles: being a critical sketch of the history of British prose fiction. By David Masson. Cambridge, 1859, 8vo.
Dickens and Thackeray, pp. 233-253.

Mateaux, C. L.—Brave Lives and Noble. By Miss C. L. Mateaux. London, 1883, 8vo.
The Boyhood of Dickens, pp. 313-320.

Mézières, L.—Histoire Critique de la Littérature Anglaise, etc.

Seconde édition. 3 tom. Paris, 1841, 8vo.
Dickens, Le Club Pickwick, tom. iii, pp. 469-496.

Nicholson, Renton.— Nicholson's Sketches of Celebrated Characters. London [1856], 8vo.
Charles Dickens. By Renton Nicholson, p. 11.

Nicoll, Henry J.—Landmarks of English Literature. By Henry J. Nicoll. London, 1883,8vo.
Dickens noticed, pp. 378-385.

Notes and Queries. General Index to Notes and Queries. Five Series. London, 1856-80, 4to.
Numerous references to C. D.

Parley.—Parley's Penny Library. London, [1841], 18mo.
Charles Dickens, with a portrait, vol i.

——Peter Parley's Annual for 1871, etc. London [1871], 8vo.
Charles Dickens as Boy and Man, pp. 320-335.

Parton, James.—Illustrious Men and their achievements; or, the people's book of biography. New York [1882], 8vo.
Charles Dickens as a Citizen, pp. 831-841.

——Some noted Princes, Authors, and Statesmen of our time. By Canon Farrar, James T. Fields, Archibald Forbes, etc. Edited by James Parton. New York [1886], 4to.
Dickens with his children, by Mamie Dickens, pp. 30-47, illustrated; Recollections of Dickens, by James T. Fields, pp. 48-51.

Payn, James.—The Youth and Middle Age of Charles Dickens. By James Payn. Edinburgh, 1883, 8vo.
Reprinted from *Chambers's Journal*, January 1872, February 1873, March 1874.

——Some literary recollections.

By James Payn. London, 1884, 8vo.
Chapter vi., First meeting with Dickens. Reprinted from *The Cornhill Magazine.*

Pemberton, T. Edgar.—Dickens's London ; or, London in the works of Charles Dickens. By T. Edgar Pemberton. London, 1876, 8vo.

Perkins, F. B.—Charles Dickens : a sketch of his life and works. By F. B. Perkins. New York, 1870, 12mo.

Pierce, Gilbert A.—The Dickens Dictionary. A key to the characters and principal incidents in the tales of Charles Dickens. By Gilbert A. Pierce. Illustrated. Boston [U.S.], 1872 12mo.

——Another edition. London, 1878, 8vo.

Poe, Edgar A.—The Literati : some honest opinions about autorial merits and demerits, etc. By Edgar A. Poe. New York, 1850, 8vo.
Notice of "Barnaby Rudge," pp. 464-482.

——The works of E. A. Poe. 4 vols. Edinburgh, 1875, 8vo.
Vol. 8, Marginalia, Dickens's "Old Curiosity Shop," and Dickens and Bulwer, pp. 373-375.

Powell, Thomas. — The Living Authors of England. By Thos. Powell. New York, 1849, 8vo.
Charles Dickens, pp. 153-178.

——Pictures of the Living Authors of Britain. By Thos. Powell. London, 1851, 8vo.
Charles Dickens, pp. 88-115.

Pryde, David.—The Genius and Writings of Charles Dickens. By David Pryde. Edinburgh, 1869, 8vo.

Reeve, Lovell A.—Portraits of men of eminence in literature,

science, and art, with biographical memoirs. [Vols.iii.-vi. by E. Walford]. 6 vols. London, 1863-67, 8vo.
Vol. iv., Charles Dickens, pp. 93-99.

Richardson, David Lester. — Literary Recreations, etc. By David Lester Richardson. London, 1852, 8vo.
Dickens's "David Copperfield,' and Thackeray's "Pendennis," pp. 238-243.

Rimmer, Alfred.—About England with Dickens. By Alfred Rimmer. With fifty-eight illustrations. London, 1883, 8vo.

Sala, Geo. A.—Charles Dickens. [An Essay.] London [1870], 8vo.

Santvoord, C. Van.—Discourses on special occasions, and miscellaneous papers. By C. Van Santvoord. New York, 1856, 8vo.
Charles Dickens and his philosophy, pp. 833-359.

Schmidt, Julian.--Charles Dickens. Eine charakteristik. Leipzig, 1852, 8vo.

Seymour, Mrs.—An account of the Origin of the "Pickwick Papers." By Mrs. Seymour, etc. London, n.d.

Shepard, William.—The Literary Life. Edited by William Shepard. Pen Pictures of Modern Authors. New York, 1882, 8vo.
Charles Dickens, pp. 236-293.

Shepherd, Richard Herne.—The Bibliography of Dickens. A bibliographical list, arranged in chronological order, of the published writings in prose and verse of Charles Dickens. From 1834 to 1880. Manchester, [1880], 8vo.

Spedding, James.—Reviews and Discussions, literary, political, and historical. By James Spedding. London, 1879, 8vo.
Dickens's "American Notes," pp. 240-276. Reprinted from the *Edinburgh Review*, Jan. 1843.

Stanley, Arthur Penrhyn. — Sermon preached in Westminster Abbey, . . . the Sunday following the funeral of Dickens. London, 1870, 8vo.

Stoddard, Richard Henry. — Bric-a-Brac Series. Anecdote Biographies of Thackeray and Dickens. Edited by Richard Henry Stoddard. New York, 1874, 8vo.

Taine, H.—Histoire de la Litterature Anglaise. Par H. Taine. 4 tom. Paris, 1864, 8vo.
Le Roman—Dickens, tom. iv., pp. 3-69.

——History of English Literature. 4 vols. Edinburgh, 1874, 8vo.
The Novel—Dickens. Vol. iv., pp. 115-164.

Taylor, Theodore. — Charles Dickens: the story of his life. New York, n.d., 8vo.

Thackeray, William Makepeace. —Early and late papers hitherto uncollected. Boston, 1867, 8vo.
Dickens in France (a description of a performance of Nicholas Nickleby in Paris), pp. 95-121. Appeared originally in *Fraser's Magazine*, March 1842.

Thomson, David Croal. — Life and Labours of Hablot Knight Browne, "Phiz." By David Croal Thomson. With one hundred and thirty illustrations, etc. London, 1884, 8vo.
Contains a series of illustrations to Dickens, printed from the original plates and blocks.

Timbs, John.—Anecdote Lives of the later wits and humourists. By John Timbs. 2 vols. London 1874, 8vo.
Vol. ii., pp. 201-255, relate to Dickens.

Times, The.—A second series of Essays from *The Times*. London, 1854, 8vo.
Dickens and Thackeray, pp. 320-338.

——Eminent Persons: biographies reprinted from the *Times*, 1870-79. London, 1880, 8vo.
Mr. Charles Dickens — Leading Article, June 10, 1870; Obituary notice, June 11, 1870, pp. 8-12.

Tooley, Mrs. G. W.—Lives, Great and Simple. London, 1884, 8vo.
Charles Dickens, pp. 183-197.

Ward, Adolphus W.—Charles Dickens. A lecture by Professor Ward. [*Science Lectures*, series 2.] Manchester, 1871, 8vo.

—— Dickens. By Adolphus William Ward. [*English Men of Letters* Series.] London, 1882, 8vo.

Watkins, William. — Charles Dickens, with anecdotes and recollections of his life. Written and compiled by William Watkins. London [1870]. 8vo.

Watt, James Crabb. — Great Novelists. Scott, Thackeray, Dickens, Lytton. By James Crabb Watt. Edinburgh, 1880, 8vo.

——Another Edition. London [1885], 8vo.

Weizmann, Louis.—Dickens und Daudet in deutscher Uebersetzung. Von Louis Weizmann. Berlin, 1880, 8vo.

Weller, Sam.—On the Origin of Sam Weller, and the real cause of the success of the Posthumous Papers of the

Pickwick Club, etc. London, 1883, 8vo.

Welsh, Alfred H.—Development of English Literature and Language. 2 vols. Chicago, 1882, 8vo.
   Dickens, vol. ii., pp. 438-454.

World. — The World's Great Men: a Gallery of over a hundred portraits and biographies, etc. London [1880], 8vo.
   Charles Dickens, with portrait, pp. 125-128.

Yates, Edmund.—Edmund Yates: his recollections and experiences. 2 vols. London, 1884, 8vo.
   A Dickens Chapter, vol. ii., pp. 91-128.

DRAMATIC.

Plays founded on Dickens's Works.

Yankee Notes for English Circulation: a farce, in one act. By E. Stirling. London, n.d., 12mo.
   Duncombe's British Theatre, vol. 46.

The Battle of Life: a drama, in three acts. By Edward Stirling. London, n.d., 12mo.
   Duncombe's British Theatre, vol. 57.

The drama founded on the Christmas Annual of Charles Dickens, called The Battle of Life: dramatized by Albert Smith. In three acts and in verse. London (1846), 12mo.

La Bataille de la Vie. Pièce en trois actes, etc. Par MM. Mélesville et André de Goy. Paris, 1853, 8vo.

Bleak House; or, Poor "Jo:" a drama, in four acts. Adapted from Dickens's "Bleak House," by George Lander. (*Dicks' Standard Plays*, No. 388.) London, n.d., 12mo.

Lady Dedlock's Secret: a drama, in four acts. Founded on an episode in Dickens's "Bleak House." By J. Palgrave Simpson. London, n.d., 8vo.

"Move On;" or, Jo, the Outcast: a drama, in three acts. Adapted by James Mortimer.
   Not published.

Poor "Jo:" a drama, in three acts. Adapted by Mr. Terry Hurst.
   Not published.

Jo: a drama, in three acts. Adapted from Charles Dickens's "Bleak House." By J. P. Burnett.
   Not published.

The Chimes: a Goblin Story. A drama, in four quarters, dramatised by Mark Lemon and Gilbert A. A'Beckett. London, n.d., 8vo.
   Webster's "Acting National Drama," vol. 11.

A Christmas Carol. By C. Z. Barnett. London (1872), 12mo.
   Lacy's Acting Edition of Plays vol 94.

The Cricket on the Hearth; or, a fairy tale of home: a drama, in three acts. Dramatized by Albert Smith (*Dicks' Standard Plays*, No. 394). London, n.d., 12mo.

The Cricket on the Hearth: a fairy tale of home. By Edward Stirling. (*Webster's "Acting National Drama,"* vol. 12.) London, n.d., 12mo.

The Cricket on the Hearth: a fairy tale of home in three chirps. By W. T. Townsend London (1860), 12mo.
   Lacy's Acting Edition of Plays, vol. 44.

Dot: a Fairy Tale of Home. A drama, in three acts. From the "Cricket on the Hearth," by Charles Dickens. Dramatized by Dion Boucicault. Not published.

David Copperfield: a drama, in three acts. Adapted from Dickens's popular work of the same name, by John Brougham. (*Dicks' Standard Plays*, No. 474.) London, n.d., 12mo.

Little Em'ly: a drama, in four acts. Adapted from Dickens's "David Copperfield," by Andrew Halliday. New York, n.d., 8vo.

Dombey and Son: in three acts. Dramatized by John Brougham. (*Dicks' Standard Plays*, No. 373.) London, n.d., 12mo.

Captain Cuttle: a comic drama, in one act. By John Brougham. (*Dicks' Standard Plays*, No. 572.) London, n.d., 12mo.

Great Expectations: a Drama, in three acts, and a prologue. Adapted by W. S. Gilbert. Not published.

The Haunted Man: a drama. Adapted from Charles Dickens's Christmas Story. Not published.

Tom Pinch: a Domestic Comedy, in three acts. Adapted by Messrs. Dilley and Clifton, from "Martin Chuzzlewit." London, n.d.

Martin Chuzzlewit: or, his Wills and his Ways, etc. A drama, in three acts. By Thomas Higgie. London [1872], 12mo. Lacy's Acting Edition, Supplement, vol. i.

Tartüffe Junior, von H. C. L. Klein. [Play in five acts, after "The Life of Martin Chuzzlewit."] Neuwied, 1864, 16mo.

Martin Chuzzlewit: a drama, in three acts. By E. Stirling. London, n.d., 12mo.

Duncombe's British Theatre, vol. 50.

Mrs. Harris! a farce, in one act. By Edward Stirling. London, n.d., 12mo. Duncombe's British Theatre, vol. 57.

Mrs. Gamp's Party. (Adapted from "Martin Chuzzlewit.") In one act. Manchester, n.d., 12mo.

Mrs. Sarah Gamp's Tea and Turn Out: a Bozzian Sketch, in one act. By B. Webster. London, n.d., 12mo. Acting National Drama, vol. xiii.

Martin Chuzzlewit: a drama, in three acts. By Charles Webb. London, n.d., 12mo.

Master Humphrey's Clock: a domestic drama, in two acts. By F. F. Cooper. (*Duncombe's British Theatre*, vol. xli.) London, n.d., 12mo.

The Old Curiosity Shop: a drama, in four acts. Adapted by Mr. Charles Dickens, Jun., from his father's novel. Not published.

Mrs. Jarley's Far-Famed Collection of Wax-Works, as arranged by G. B. Bartlett. In two parts. London [1873], 8vo.

The Old Curiosity Shop: a drama, in four acts. Adapted from Charles Dickens's novel of the same name, by George Lander. (*Dicks' Standard Plays*, No. 398.) London, n.d., 12mo.

The Old Curiosity Shop: a drama, in two acts. By E. Stirling. London [1868], 12mo. Lacy's Acting Edition of Plays, vol. lxxvii.

Barnaby Rudge: a drama, in three acts. Adapted from Dickens's work by Thomas Higgie. London [1854], 12mo.

Barnaby Rudge: a domestic

diama, in three acts. By Charles Selby and Charles Melville. London [1875], 12mo.

Lacy's Acting Edition of Plays, vol. ci.

A Message from the Sea : a drama, in four acts. Founded on Charles Dickens's tale of that name. By John Brougham. (*Dicks' Standard Plays*, No. 459.) London, n.d., 12mo.

A Message from the Sea : a drama, in three acts. By Charles Dickens and William Wilkie Collins. London, 1861, 8vo.

The Infant Phenomenon, etc. : a domestic piece, in one act. Being an episode in the adventures of "Nicholas Nickleby." Adapted by H. Horncastle. London, n.d., 8vo.

Nicholas Nickleby : a drama, in four acts. Adapted by H. Simms. (*Dicks' Standard Plays*, No. 469.) London, n.d., 12mo.

The Fortunes of Smike, or a Sequel to Nicholas Nickleby : a drama, in two acts. By Edward Stirling. London, n.d., 12mo.

Webster's "National Acting Drama," vol. ix.

Nicholas Nickleby : a farce, in two acts. By Edward Stirling. London, n.d., 12mo.

Webster's "Acting National Drama," vol v.

Nicholas Nickleby : an Episodic Sketch, in three tableaux, based upon an incident in "Nicholas Nickleby."

Not published.

L'Abîme, drame en cinq actes. [Founded on the story of "No Thoroughfare."] Paris, 1868, 8vo.

No Thorough Fare : a drama, in five acts, and a prologue. By

Charles Dickens and Wilkie Collins. New York, n.d., 8vo.

Identity ; or, No Thoroughfare. A drama, in four acts. By Louis Lequêl. New York, n.d., 8vo.

Bumble's Courtship. From Dickens's "Oliver Twist." A Comic Interlude, in one act. By Frank E. Emson. London [1874], 12mo.

Lacy's Acting Edition of Plays, vol. xcix.

Oliver Twist : a serio-comic burletta, in three acts. By George Almar. London, n.d., 12mo.

Webster's "Acting National Drama," vol. vi.

Oliver Twist, or the Parish Boy's Progress : a domestic drama, in three acts. By C. Z. Barnett. London, n.d., 12mo.

Duncombe's British Theatre, vol. xxix.

Oliver Twist : a serio-comic burletta, in four acts. By George Almar. New York, n.d.

Sam Weller, or the Pickwickians: a drama, in three acts, etc. By W. T. Moncrieff. London, 1837, 8vo.

The Pickwickians, or the Peregrinations of Sam Weller : a Comic Drama, in three acts. Arranged from Moncrieff's adaptation of Charles Dickens's work, by T. H. Lacy. London [1837], 8vo.

The Great Pickwick Case, arranged as a comic operetta. The words of the songs by Robert Pollitt ; the music arranged by Thomas Rawson. Manchester [1884], 8vo.

The Pickwick Club . . . a burletta, in three acts. By E. Stirling. London [1837], 12mo.

Duncombe's British Theatre, vol. xxvi.

The Peregrinations of Pickwick: an acting drama. By William Leman Rede. London, 1837, 8vo.

Bardell *versus* Pickwick ; versified and diversified. Songs and choruses. Words by T. H. Gem ; music by Frank Spinney. · Leamington [1881], 12mo.

The Dead Witness ; or Sin and its Shadow. A drama, in three acts, founded on " The Widow's Story " of The Seven Poor Travellers, by Charles Dickens. The drama written by Wybert Reeve. London [1874], 12mo.
Lacy's Acting Edition of Plays vol. xcix.

A Tale of Two Cities : a drama, in two acts, etc. By Tom Taylor. London [1860], 12mo.
Lacy's Acting Edition of Plays, vol. xlv.

The Tale of Two Cities : a drama, in three acts. Adapted by H. J. Rivers, etc. London [1862], 12mo.

MUSICAL.

All the Year Round ; or, The Search for Happiness. A song. Words by W. S. Passmore ; music by John J. Blockley. London [1860], fol.

Yankee Notes for English Circulation ; or, Boz in A-Merry-Key. Comic song, by J. Briton. Music by Loder. [1842.]

Dolly Varden : a Ballad. Words and music by Cotsford Dick. London [1880], fol.

Maypole Hugh : a song. Words by Charles Bradberry ; music by George E. Fox. London [1881], fol.

The Chimes Quadrille. (*Musical Bouquet*, No. 5.) London, n.d., fol.

The Cricket on the Hearth: Quad-

rille. By F. Lancelott. (*Musical Bouquet*, No. 57.) London [1846], fol.

What are the Wild Waves Saying ? A vocal duet. Written by Joseph E. Carpenter ; music by Stephen Glover. London [1850], fol.

A Voice from the Waves: a vocal duet, in answer to the above. Words by R. Ryan ; music by Stephen Glover. London [1850], fol.

Little Dorrit's Vigil. A Song. Written by John Barnes ; composed by George Linley. London [1856], fol.

Who Passes by this Road so Late ? Blandois' song, from " Little Dorrit." Words by Charles Dickens. Music by H. R. S. Dalton. London [1857], fol.

My Dear Old Home : a ballad. Words by J. E. Carpenter. Music by John J. Blockley. [Founded on Dickens's " Little Dorrit."] London [1857], fol.

Floating Away : a ballad. Words by J. E. Carpenter. Music by John J. Blockley. [Founded on a passage in " Little Dorrit."] London [1857], fol.

The Nicholas Nickleby Quadrilles and Nickleby Galop. By Sydney Vernon. London, 1839, fol.

Little Nell : a melody. Composed by George Linley, and arranged for the pianoforte by Carlo Zotti. London [1865], fol.

The Ivy Green : a song. Music by Mrs. Henry Dale. London [1840], fol.
The song is introduced in chap. vi. of the " Pickwick Papers" as a

recitation by the clergyman of Dingley Dell.
The Ivy Green : a song. Music by A. De Belfour. London [1843], fol.
The Ivy Green. Arranged for the pianoforte by Ricardo Linter. London [1844], fol.
The Ivy Green : a song. Music by Henry Russell. London [1844], fol.
The Ivy Green. Music by W. Lovell Phillips. London [1844], fol.
Gabriel Grub. Cantata Seria Buffa. Adapted from "Pickwick." Music by George E. Fox. London [1881], 4to.
Sam Weller's Adventures : a song of the Pickwickians (Reprinted in *The Life and Times of James Catnach*, by Charles Hindley. (London, 1878).
The Tuggs's at Ramsgate. Versified from "Boz's" sketch.
The Child and the Old Man : song in the Opera, "The Village Coquettes." The words by Charles Dickens, the music by John Hullah. London [1836], fol.
Love is not a feeling to pass away : a ballad in "The Village Coquettes." Words by C. Dickens. Music by John Hullah. London [1836], fol.
My Fair Home : air in "The Village Coquettes." Words by Charles Dickens. Music by John Hullah. London [1836], fol.
No light bound of stag or timid hare. Quintett in the Opera, "The Village Coquettes." The words by Charles Dickens, the music by John Hullah. London [1836], fol.

Some Folks who have grown old. Song in "The Village Coquettes." Words by Charles Dickens. Music by John Hullah. London [1836], fol.
There's a Charm in Spring : a ballad in "The Village Coquettes." Words by Charles Dickens. Music by John Hullah. London [1836], fol.
The Cares of the Day : song with chorus, in the Opera, "The Village Coquettes." The words by Charles Dickens, composed by John Hullah. London [1858], fol.
In Rich and Lowly Station shine. Duet in the Opera, "The Village Coquettes." The words by Charles Dickens, the music by John Hullah. London [1858], fol.
Autumn Leaves : air from the Opera, "The Village Coquettes." The words by Charles Dickens, the music by John Hullah. London [1871], fol.

PARODIES AND IMITATIONS.

Change for the American Notes ; or, Letters from London to New York. By an American Lady. London, 1843, 8vo.
Current American Notes. By "Buz." London, n.d.
The Battle of London Life ; or, "Boz" and his Secretary. By Morna. With a portrait and illustrations by G. A. Sala. London, 1849.
The Battle Won by the Wind. By Ch—s D*ck*ns, etc. Published in *The Puppet Showman's Album*. Illustrated by Gavarni.
Bleak House : a Narrative of Real Life, etc. London, 1856.

Characteristic Sketches of Young Gentlemen. By Quiz Junior. With woodcut illustrations. London [1838].

A Child's History of Germany. By H. W. Friedlaender. A Pendant to a Child's History of England, by Charles Dickens. Celle, 1861, 8vo.

" Christmas Eve " with the Spirits . . . with some further tidings of the Lives of Scrooge and Tiny Tim. London, 1870.

A Christmas Carol : being a few scattered staves, from a familiar composition, re-arranged for performance, by a distinguished Musical Amateur, during the holiday season, at H—rw—rd—n. With four illustrations by Harry Furness.
  Punch, Dec. 1885, pp. 304, 305.

Micawber Redivivus ; or, How to Make a Fortune as a Middleman, etc. By Jonathan Coalfield [*i.e.* W. Graham Simpson ?]. [London, 1833], 8vo.

Dombey and Son Finished : a burlesque. Illustrated by Albert Smith.
  The Man in the Moon, 1848, pp. 59-67.

Dombey and Daughter : a moral fiction. By Renton Nicholson. London [1850], 8vo.

Dolby and Father, by Buz. [A satire on C. Dickens.] New York, 1868, 12mo.

Hard Times (Refinished). By Charles Diggens.
  Parody on *Hard Times*, published in " Our Miscellany." Edited by H. Yates and R. B. Brough, pp. 142-156.

The Haunted Man. By CH—R—S D—C—K—N—S. New York, 1870, 12mo.
  Condensed Novels, and Other Papers. By F. Bret Harte.

Mister Humfries' Clock. " Bos," Maker. A miscellany of striking interest. Illustrated. London, 1840, 8vo.

Master Timothy's Bookcase ; or, the Magic Lanthorn of the World. By G. W. M. Reynolds. London, 1842.

A Girl at a Railway Junction's Reply [to an article in the Christmas number for 1866 of " All the Year Round," entitled " Mugby Junction."] London [1867], 8vo.

The Cloven Foot : being an adaptation of the English novel, " The Mystery of Edwin Drood " to American scenes, characters, customs, and nomenclature. By Orpheus C. Kerr. New York, 1870, 8vo.

The Mystery of Mr. E. Drood. By Orpheus C. Kerr.
  The Piccadilly Annual, Dec. 1870, pp. 59-62.

The Mystery of Mr. E. Drood. An adaptation. By O. C. Kerr. London [1871], 8vo.

John Jasper's Secret : a sequel to Charles Dickens's unfinished novel, " The Mystery of Edwin Drood." Philadelphia [1871].

The Mystery of Edwin Drood. Part the Second, by the Spirit Pen of Charles Dickens, etc. Brattleboro' [U.S.], 1873.

A Great Mystery Solved : being a sequel to " The Mystery of Edwin Drood." By Gillan Vase. 3 vols. London, 1878, 8vo.

Nicholas Nickelbery. Containing the adventures of the family of Nickelbery. By " Bos." With forty-three woodcut illustrations. London [1838], 8vo.

Scenes from the Life of Nickleby Married . . . being a sequel to the "Life and Adventures of Nicholas Nickleby." Edited by "Guess." With twenty-one etched illustrations by "Quiz." London, 1840.

No Thoroughfare : the Book in Eight Acts, etc.
The Mask. February 1868, pp. 14-18.

No Throughfare. [A Parody upon Dickens's " No Thorough-fare."] By C—s D—s, B. Brownjohn, and Domby. Second Edition. Boston [U.S.], 1868, 8vo.

The Life and Adventures of Oliver Twiss, the Workhouse Boy. [Edited by Bos.] London [1839]. 8vo.

Posthumous Papers of the Cadger's Club. With sixteen engrav-ings. London [1837].

Posthumous Papers of the Won-derful Discovery Club, formerly of Camden Town. Established by Sir Peter Patron. Edited by "Poz." With eleven illustra-tions, designed by Squib, and engraved by Point. London, 1838.

The Post-humourous Notes of the Pickwickian Club. Edited by "Bos." Illustrated with 120 engravings. 2 vols. London [1839], 8vo.
There are, in fact, 332 engravings.

Pickwick in America ! detailing all the . . . adventures of taat [*sic.*] individual in the United States. Edited by " Bos." Illustrated with forty-six engravings. London [1840], 8vo.

Pickwick Abroad ; or, the Tour in France. By George W. M. Reynolds. Illustrated with forty-one steel plates, by Alfred Crowquill, etc. London, 1839, 8vo.
——Another edition. London, 1864, 8vo.

Lloyd's Pickwickian Songster, etc. London [1837].

Pickwick Songster. With por-traits, designed by C. J. Grant,. of "Mr. Pickwick as Apollo," and "Sam Weller brushing boots." London, n.d.

The Pickwick Comic Almanac for 1838. With twelve comic woodcut illustrations, drawn by R. Cruikshank. London, 1838.

Mr. Pickwick's Collection of Songs. Illustrated. London [1837], 12mo.

Pickwick Treasury of Wit ; or, Joe Miller's Jest Book. Dublin, 1840.

Sam Weller's Favourite Song Book. London [1837], 12mo.

Sam Weller's Pickwick Jest-Book, etc. With illustrations by Cruikshank, and portraits of all the " Pickwick " characters. London, 1837.

The Sam Weller Scrap Sheet. With forty woodcut portraits of "all the Pickwick Char-acters," etc. London, n.d.

Facts and Figures from Italy. Addressed during the last two winters to C. Dickens, being an appendix to his " Pictures." By Don Jeremy Savonarola. London, 1847, 8vo.

The Sketch Book. By " Bos." Containing tales, sketches, etc. With seventeen woodcut illus-trations. London [1837], 8vo.

POETICAL.

Impromptu. By C. J. Davids.
Bentley's Miscellany, No. 2,
March 1837, p. 297.

Poetical Epistle from Father
Prout to "Boz." A poem of
seven verses.
Bentley's Miscellany, Jan. 1838, p. 71.

A Tribute to Charles Dickens. A
poem of twelve lines. By the
Hon. Mrs. Norton.
English Bijou Almanac, 1842.

To Charles Dickens on his proposed voyage to America, 1842.
By Thomas Hood.
New Monthly Magazine, Feb.
1842, p. 217.

To Charles Dickens, on his
"Christmas Carol." A poem
of fifteen lines. By W. W. G.
Illuminated Magazine, Feb. 1844,
p. 189.

To Charles Dickens on his
"Oliver Twist." By T. N.
Talfourd.
*Tragedies; to which are added a
few Sonnets and Verses,* by T. N.
Talfourd, p. 244. London, 1844.
16mo.

The American's Apostrophe to
"Boz." A poem.
*The Book of Ballads [by T. Martin
and W. E. Aytoun].* Edited by Bon
Gaultier, pp. 81-86. London, 1845,
16mo.

To Charles Dickens. A Sonnet.
*Douglas Jerrold's Shilling Maga-
zine,* March 1845, p. 250.

To Charles Dickens. A Dedi-
catory Sonnet. By John
Forster.
*The Life and Adventures of Oliver
Goldsmith,* by John Forster. Lon-
don, 1848, 8vo.

To Charles Dickens. A Dedi-
catory Poem of two verses. By
James Ballantine.
Poems, by James Ballantine.
Edinburgh, 1856, 8vo.

Au Revoir. A poem of four
verses.
Judy, Oct. 30, 1867, p. 37.

A Welcome to Dickens. A poem
of eighty-four lines. By F. J.
Parmentier.
Harper's Weekly, Nov. 30, 1867,
pp. 757, 758.

Impromptu. A Humorous Verse
of six lines.
Life of Charles Dickens, by R.
Shelton Mackenzie, p. 97. Philadelphia [1870], 8vo.

Charles Dickens reading to his
daughters on the Lawn at
Gadshill. A poem of eight
verses. By the Editor
(C. W.).
Life, Dec. 8, 1880, p. 1005.

Memorial Verses, June 9, 1870.
Fifteen verses. By F. T. P.
Daily News, June 18, 1870, p. 5.

Ode to the Memory of Charles
Dickens. By A. B. Hume.
*A Christmas Memorial of Charles
Dickens,* by A. B. Hume. London,
1870, 8vo.

Charles Dickens. Born February
7, 1812. Died June 9, 1870.
A memorial poem of fourteen
verses.
Punch, June 18, 1870, p. 244.

In Memoriam. June 9, 1870. A
poem of six verses.
Graphic, June 18, 1870, p. 678.

Charles Dickens. Born 7th February 1812; died 9th June
870. A memorial sonnet.
Judy, June 22, 1870, p. 91.

In Memory. A poem of ten
verses, with an illustration by
F. Barnard.
Fun, June 25, 1870, p. 157.

In Memoriam. A poem of seventy
lines. By H. M. C.
Gentleman's Magazine, July 1,
1870, p. 22.

To His Memory. A poem of five
verses.
Argosy, August, 1870, p. 114.

A Man of the Crowd to Charles
Dickens. A poem of a hundred-

and-six lines. By E. J. Milliken.
Gentleman's Magazine, August 1870, pp. 277-279.

Dickens. A memorial poem of two verses. By O. C. K. (Orpheus C. Kerr).
Piccadilly Annual, Dec. 1870, p. 72.

In Memoriam. Charles Dickens. *Obiit,* June 9, 1870. Five verses.
Charles Dickens, with anecdotes and recollections of his life. By William Watkins. London [1870], 8vo.

Dickens in Camp. A poem of ten verses. By F. Bret Harte.
Poems, by F. Bret Harte. Boston, 1871, 12mo.

Dickens at Gadshill. A poem of eighteen verses. By C. K. (Charles Kent).
Athenæum, June 3, 1871, p. 687.

Death of Charles Dickens. A poem of seventeen verses.
The Circe and other Poems, by John Appleby, 1873.

At Gad's Hill. An obituary poem of fourteen verses. By Richard Henry Stoddard.
Bric-a-Brac Series. Anecdote Biographies of Thackeray and Dickens, p. 296. By Richard Henry Stoddard. New York, 1874, 8vo.

At the Grave of Dickens. A sonnet. By Clelia R. Crespi.
Detroit Free Press, July 1894.

In Memoriam : Charles Dickens. Died June 9, 1870. A sonnet. By C. K.
Graphic, June 6, 1885, p. 586.

MAGAZINE AND NEWSPAPER ARTICLES.

Charles Dickens. *Revue Britannique,* Avril 1843, pp. 340-376. —*People's Journal* (portrait), by William Howitt, 1846, vol. 1, pp. 8-12.—*Revue des Deux Mondes,* by Arthur Dudley, March 1848, pp. 901-922.—

Dickens, Charles.

Blackwood's Edinburgh Magazine, April 1855, pp. 451-466 ; same article, *Eclectic Magazine,* June 1855, pp. 200-214.—*Die Gartenlaube* (portrait), 1856, pp. 73-75.—*Saturday Review,* May 1858, pp. 474, 475 ; same article, *Littell's Living Age,* July 1858, pp. 263-265 —*Town Talk,* June 1858, p. 76.—*National Review,* vol. 7, 1858, pp. 458-486.—*Illustrated News of the World,* Supplement, Oct. 9, 1858.—*National Review* (by W. Bagehot), Oct. 1858, pp. 458-486 ; same article, *Littell's Living Age,* 1858, pp. 643-659 ; and in "Literary Studies by the late Walter Bagehot."—*Critic* (portrait), 1858, pp. 534-537.—*Harper's New Monthly Magazine,* 1862, pp. 376 380.—*Every Saturday,* vol. 1, 1866, p. 79 ; vol. 9, p. 225.—*Harper's Weekly* (portrait), 1867, p. 757 ; same article, *Littell's Living Age,* 1867, pp. 688-690.—*North American Review,* by C. E. Norton, April, 1868, pp. 671-672.—*Court Suburb Magazine,* by B., Dec. 1868, pp. 142, 143. —*Contemporary Review,* by George Stott, Feb. 1869, pp. 203-225 ; same article, *Littell's Living Age,* March 1869, pp. 707-720.—*L'Illustration* (portrait), by Jules Claretie, 18 Juin, 1870—*Le Monde Illustré* (portrait), by Léo de Bernard, 25 Juin, 1870.—*Annual Register,* 1870, pp. 151-153.—*Illustrated London News* (portrait), June, 1870, p. 639.—*Spectator,* 1870, pp. 716, 717.—*Ueber Land und Meer* (portrait), No.

Dickens, Charles.

42, 1870, p. 19.—*Fraser's Magazine*, July 1870, pp. 130-134.—*Putnam's Monthly Magazine*, by P. Godwin, vol. 16, 1870, p. 231.—*St. Paul's Magazine*, by Anthony Trollope, July 1870, pp. 370-375; same article, *Eclectic Magazine*, Sept. 1870, pp. 297-301.—*Illustrated Magazine*, by "Meteor," 1870, pp. 164, 165.—*Illustrated Review*, with portrait, vol. 1, 1870, pp. 1-4.—*Hours at Home*, by D. G. Mitchell, 1870, pp. 363-368.—*Gentleman's Magazine* (portrait), July 1870, pp. 21, 22.—*Graphic* (portrait), 1870, p. 687.—*Nation* (by J. R. Dennett), 1870, pp. 380, 381.—*Temple Bar*, by Alfred Austin, July 1870, pp. 554-562.—*St James's Magazine* (portrait), 1870, pp. 696-699.—*Victoria Magazine*, by Edward Roscoe, vol. 15, 1870, pp. 357-363.—*Art Journal*, July, 1870, p. 224.—*Leisure Hour* (portrait), by Miss E. J. Whately, Nov. 1870, pp. 728-732. — *New Eclectic*, by B. Jerrold, vol. 7, 1871, p. 332.—*London Quarterly Review*, Jan. 1871, pp. 265-286.—*Blackwood's Edinburgh Magazine*, June 1871, pp. 673-695; same article, *Eclectic Magazine*, Sept. 1871, pp. 257, 274; *Littell's Living Age*, July 1871, pp. 29-44.—*Gentleman's Magazine*, by George Barnett Smith, 1874, pp. 301-316.—*Social Notes*, by Moy Thomas (portrait), etc., Oct. 1879, pp. 114-117.—*Fortnightly Review*, by Mowbray Morris, Dec. 1882, pp. 762-779.

Dickens, Charles.

——About England with. *Scribner's Monthly*, by R. E. Martin [illustrated], Aug. 1880, pp. 494-503.
——Amateur Theatricals. *Macmillan's Magazine*, Jan. 1871, pp. 206-215; same article, *Eclectic Magazine*, March 1871, pp. 322-330.—*Every Saturday*, vol. 10, p. 70.
——As "Captain Bobadil" (portrait). *Every Saturday*, vol. 11, p. 295.
——American Notes. *Fraser's Magazine*, Nov. 1842, pp. 617-629. — *Monthly Review*, Nov. 1842, pp. 392-403.—*Chambers's Edinburgh Journal*, Nov. 1842, pp. 348, 349, 356, 357.—*New Monthly Magazine* (by Thomas Hood), Nov. 1842, pp. 396-406. — *Blackwood's Edinburgh Magazine*, by Q. Q. Q., Dec. 1842, pp. 783-801.—*Tait's Edinburgh Magazine*, vol. 9, 1842, pp. 737-746.—*Christian Remembrancer*, Dec. 1842, pp. 679, 680.—*Edinburgh Review*, by James Spedding, Jan. 1843, pp. 497-522. Reprinted in "Reviews and Discussions," etc., by James Spedding; Note to the above, Feb. 1843, p. 301.—*Eclectic Museum*, vol. 1, 1843, p. 230.—*North American Review*, Jan. 1843, pp. 212-237.—*Quarterly Review*, March 1843, pp. 502-522. —*Westminster Review*, by H., 1843, pp. 146-160.—*New Englander*, by J. P. Thompson, 1843, pp. 64-84.—*Southern Literary Messenger*, 1843, pp. 58-62.—*Atlantic Monthly*, by Edwin P. Whipple, April 1877, pp. 462-466.

Dickens, Charles.

——And Benjamin Disraeli. *Tailor and Cutter*, July 1870, pp. 401-402.

——The Styles of Disraeli and. *Galaxy*, by Richard Grant White, Aug. 1870, pp. 253-263.

——And Thackeray. *Littell's Living Age*, vol. 21, p. 224.—*Dublin Review*, April 1871, pp. 315-350.

——And Bulwer. A Contrast. *Temple Bar*, Jan. 1875, pp. 168-180.

——Living Literati ; Sir E. Bulwer Lytton and Mr. Charles Dickens. *Eginton's Literary Railway Miscellany*, 1854, pp. 19-25, 174-188.

——And Chauncy Hare Towns-hend. *London Society*, Aug. 1870, pp. 157-159.

——And his Critics. *The Train*, by John Hollingshead, Aug. 1857, pp. 76-79; reprinted in "Essays and Miscellanies" by John Hollingshead.

——And his Debt of Honour. *Land We Love*, vol. 5, p. 414.

——And his Illustrators. With nine illustrations. *Christmas Bookseller*, 1879, pp. 15-21.

——And his Letters. Part 1. By Mary Cowden Clarke. *Gentleman's Magazine*, Dec. 1876, pp. 708-713.

——And his Works. *Fraser's Magazine*, April 1840, pp. 381-400.

——Another Gossip about.—*Englishwoman's Domestic Magazine*, vol. 12, 1872, pp. 78-83.

——As an Author and Reader. *Welcome*, with portrait, vol. 12, 1885, pp. 166-170.

Dickens, Charles.

——As a Dramatic Critic. *Long-man's Magazine*, by Dutton Cook, May 1883, pp. 29-42.

——As a Dramatist and a Poet. *Gentleman's Magazine*, by Percy Fitzgerald, 1878, pp. 61-77.

——As a Humaniser. *St. James's Magazine*, by Arnold Quamo-clit, 1879, pp. 281-291.

——As a Journalist. *Journalist, A Monthly Phonographic Maga-zine*, by Charles Kent, in Pit-man's Shorthand, vol. 1, Dec. 1879, pp. 17-25. Done into English—*Time*, July 1881, pp. 361-374.

——As a Literary Exemplar. *University Quarterly*, by F. A. Walker, vol. 1, p. 91, etc.

——As a Moralist. *Old and New*, April 1871, pp. 480-483.

——As a Moral Teacher. *Monthly Religious Magazine*, by J. H. Morison, vol. 44, p. 129, etc.

——As a Reader. *The Critic*, 1858, pp. 537, 538.

——Eine Vorlesung von Charles Dickens. *Die Gartenlaube*, by Corvin (portrait), 1861, pp. 612-614.

——Readings by Charles Dickens. *Land We Love*, by T. C. Du Leon, vol. 4, p. 421, etc.

——Farewell Reading in London. *Every Saturday*, vol. 9, pp 242, 260.

——Last Readings. *Graphic*, February 1870, p. 250.

——New Reading. Illustrated. *Tinsley's Magazine*, by Edmund Yates, 1869, pp. 60-64.

——At Home. *Every Saturday*, vol. 2, p. 396. *Gentleman's Magazine* (by Percy Fitz-gerald), November 1881, pp. 562-583. — *Cornhill Magazine*

Dickens, Charles.

(by his eldest daughter), 1885, pp. 32-51.

——At Gadshill Place. *Life,* 1880, pp. 1005, 1006.

——Biographical Sketch of. *The Eclectic Magazine* (portrait), 1864, pp. 115-117.

——Bleak House. *Rambler,* vol. 1. N.S., 1854, pp. 41-45.

——Boyhood of. *Thistle,* by J. D. D., vol. 1, pp. 51-55.

——Childhood of. (Illustrated.) *Manchester Quarterly,* by Robert L. Langton, vol. 1, 1882, pp. 178-180.

——Early Life of. *Every Saturday,* vol. 12, p. 60.

——Boz. *The Englishwoman's Domestic Magazine,* by J. T., July 1870, pp. 14-16.

——The "Boz" Ball. *Historical Magazine,* by P. M., pp. 110-113 and 291-294.

——"Boz" in Paris.—*Englishwoman's Domestic Magazine,* vol. 10, pp. 186-189.

——Boz *versus* Dickens. *Parker's London Magazine,* February 1845, pp. 122-128.

——Grip the Raven, in "Barnaby Rudge." *Every Saturday,* vol. 9, 542, 742, 749.

——The Battle of Life. *Tait's Edinburgh Magazine,* 1847, pp. 55-60.

——Bleak House. *Spectator* (by George Brimley), Sep. 1853, pp. 923-925. Reprinted in " Essays by the late George Brimley."— *United States Magazine and Democratic Review,* Sep. 1853, pp. 276-280.—*North American Review* (by W. Sargent,) Oct. 1853, pp. 409-439.—*Eclectic Review,* Dec. 1853, pp. 665-679.

Dickens, Charles.

—— ——Characters in. *Putnam's Monthly Magazine* (by C. F. Riggs), 1853, pp. 558-562.

——Characters from Dickens [Illustrated]. *Jack and Jill,* 1885-6.

——The Chimes. *Dublin Review,* Dec. 1844, pp. 560-568.— *Eclectic Review,* 1845, pp. 70-88. —*Edinburgh Review,* Jan. 1845, pp. 181-189; same article, *Eclectic Magazine,* May 1845, pp. 33-38.

——Christmas Books. *Union Magazine,* Feb. 1846, pp. 223-236.

——A Christmas Carol. *Dublin Review,* 1843, pp. 510-529.— *Fraser's Magazine,* by M. A. T., Feb. 1844, pp. 167-169.—*Hood's Magazine,* 1844, pp. 68-75.— *Knickerbocker,* by S. G. Clark, March, 1844, pp. 276-281.

——Controversy. *American Publishers' Circular,* June 1867, pp. 68-69.

——Cricket on the Hearth. *Chambers's Edinburgh Journal,* 1846, pp. 44-48.—*Oxford and Cambridge Review,* vol. 2, 1846, pp. 43-50.

——David Copperfield. *Fraser's Magazine,* Dec. 1850, pp. 698-710; same article, *Eclectic Magazine,* Feb. 1851, pp. 247-258.

——David Copperfield and Arthur Pendennis. *Southern Literary Messenger,* 1851, pp. 499-504.—*Prospective Review,* July 1851, pp. 157-191.—*North British Review* (by David Masson), May 1851, pp. 57-89; same article, *Littell's Living Age,* July 1851, pp. 97-110.

—— ——Schools; or, Teachers and Taught. *Family Herald,* July 1849, pp. 204-205.

Dickens, Charles.

——The Death of. Articles reprinted from the *Saturday Review*, the *Spectator*, the *Daily News*, and the *Times*. *Eclectic Magazine*, Aug. 1870, pp. 217-224.—*Saturday Review*, June 11, 1870, pp. 760, 761.—*Every Saturday*, vol. 9, 1870, p. 450.

——Devonshire House Theatricals. *Bentley's Miscellany*, 1851, pp. 660-667.

——Dictionary of (Pierce and Wheeler's). *Every Saturday*, vol. 11, p. 258.

——Dogs ; or, the Landseer of Fiction. [Illustrated.] *London Society*, July 1863, pp. 48-61.

——Dombey and Son. *Chambers's Edinburgh Journal*. Oct. 1846, pp. 269, 270.—*North British Review*, May 1847, pp. 110-136.—*Rambler*, vol. 1, 1848, pp. 64, 66.—*Sun* (by Charles Kent), April 13, 1848.

—— ——Humourists : Dickens and Thackeray (Dombey and Son and Vanity Fair). *English Review*, Dec. 1848, pp. 257-275 ; same article, *Eclectic Magazine*, March 1849, pp. 370-379.

—— ——The Wooden Midshipman (of " Dombey and Son "). (By Ashby Sterry.) *All the Year Round*, Oct. 1881, pp. 173-179.

——English Magazines on, 1870. *Every Saturday*, vol. 9, p. 482.

——Farewell Banquet to, 1867. *Every Saturday*, vol. 4, p. 705.

——A Few Words on. *Town and Country*, by A. J. H. Crespi, N.S., vol. 1. 1873, pp. 265-273.

——Footprints of. *Harper's New Monthly Magazine*, by M. D. Conway. 1870, pp. 610-616.

Dickens, Charles.

——Forster's Life of (Vol. 1). *Examiner*, by Herbert Wilson, Dec. 1871, pp. 1217, 1218 ; same article, *Eclectic Magazine*, Feb. 1872, pp. 237-240. — *Chambers's Journal* (by James Payn), Jan. 1872, pp. 17-21 and 40-45.—*Quarterly Review*, Jan. 1872, pp. 125-147. — *Nation*, 1872, pp. 42, 43.—*Fortnightly Review*, by J. Herbert Stack, Jan. 1872, pp. 117-120.— *Fraser's Magazine*, Jan. 1872, pp. 105-113 ; same article, *Eclectic Magazine*, March 1872, pp 277-284. — *Canadian Monthly*, Feb. 1872, pp. 179-182.—*Lakeside Monthly*, April 1872, pp. 336-340. — *Overland Monthly*, by George B. Merrill, May 1872, pp. 443-451.

——Forster's Life of (vol. 2). *Examiner*, Nov. 1872, pp. 1132, 1133.—*Nation*, 1873, pp. 28, 29. —*Chambers's Journal* (by James Payn), Feb. 1873, pp. 74-79.— *Canadian Monthly*, Feb. 1873, pp. 171-173.—*Temple Bar*, May 1873, pp. 169-185.

——Forster's Life of (vol. 3). *Examiner*, 1874, pp. 161, 162.— *Nation*, 1874, pp. 175, 176.— *Chambers's Journal* (by James Payn), March 1874, pp. 177-180. —*Canadian Monthly*, April 1874, pp. 364-366.

——Forster's Life of. *International Review*, May 1874, pp. 417-420.—*North American Review*, vol. 114, p. 413.—*Every Saturday*, vol. 14, p. 608.— *Revue des Deux Mondes*, by Léon Boucher, tom. 8, 1875, pp. 95-126.—*American Bibliopolist*, vol. 4, p. 125.—*Catholic World*, by J. R. G. Hassard, vol. 30, p. 692.

Dickens, Charles.

——Four months with. (1842.) *Atlantic Monthly*, by G. W. Putnam. 1870, pp. 476-482, 591-599.

——French Criticism of. *People's Journal*, vol. 5, p. 228.

——On the Genius of. *Knickerbocker*, by F. W. Shelton, May 1852, pp. 421-431.—*Putnam's Monthly Magazine*, by G. F. Talbot, 1855, pp. 263-272.—*Atlantic Monthly*, by E. P. Whipple, May 1867, pp. 546-554.—*Spectator*, 1870, pp. 749-751.—*New Eclectic*, vol. 7, 1871, p. 257

——The "Good Genie" of Fiction. *St. Paul's Magazine*, by Robert Buchanan, 1872, pp. 130-148; reprinted in "A Poet's Sketch-Book," etc., by Robert Buchanan, 1883.

——Great Expectations. *Atlantic Monthly*, by Edwin P. Whipple, Sep. 1877, pp. 327-333.—*Eclectic Review*, Oct. 1861, pp. 458-477.—*Dublin University Magazine*, Dec. 1861, pp. 685-693.

——Bygone Celebrities: I. The Guild of Literature and Art. *Gentleman's Magazine*, by R. H. Horne, Feb. 1871, pp. 247-262.

——Hard Times. *Westminster Review*, Oct. 1854, pp. 604-608.—*Atlantic Monthly*, by Edwin P. Whipple, March 1877, pp. 353-358.

——The Home of. *Hours at Home*, by John D. Sherwood, July 1867, pp. 239-242.—*Every Saturday*, vol. 9, p. 228.

——In and Out of London with. *Scribner's Monthly*, by B. E.

Dickens, Charles.

Martin. [Illustrated.] May 1881, pp. 32-45.

——In London with. *Scribner's Monthly*, by B. E. Martin. (Illustrated). March 1881, pp. 649-664.

——In the Editor's Chair. *Gentleman's Magazine*, by Percy Fitzgerald, June 1881, pp. 725-742.

——In Memoriam. By A. H. (Arthur Helps). *Macmillan's Magazine*, July 1870, pp. 236-240. — *Gentleman's Magazine*, by Blanchard Jerrold, July 1870, pp. 228-241; reprinted, with additions, as "A Day with Charles Dickens," in the "Best of all Good Company," by Blanchard Jerrold, 1872.

——In New York (by J. R. Dennett). *Nation*, 1867, pp. 482, 483.

——In Poet's Corner. *Illustrated London News*, June 1870, pp. 652 and 662, 663.

——In Relation to Christmas. *Graphic* Christmas Number, 1870, p. 19.

——In Relation to Criticism. *Fortnightly Review*, by George Henry Lewes. 1872, pp. 141-154; same article, *Eclectic Magazine*, 1872, pp. 445-453; *Every Saturday*, vol. 12., p. 246, etc.

——A Lost Work of (Is She His Wife? or, Something Singular). *The Pen; a Journal of Literature*, by Richard Herne Shepherd, October 1880, pp. 311, 312.

——Least known writings of. *Every Saturday*, vol. 9, p. 471.

——Letters of. *Fortnightly Review*, by William Minto, Dec. 1879, pp. 845-862; same article, *Littell's Living Age*, 1880, pp.

Dickens, Charles.

3-13 ; *Eclectic Magazine*, 1880, pp. 165-175.—*Nation*, by W. C. Brownell, December 1879, pp. 388-390.—*Literary World*, December 1879, pp. 369-371. —*Scribner's Monthly*, Jan. 1880, pp. 470, 471.—*Appleton's Journal of Literature*, 1880, pp. 72-81.—*Contemporary Review*, by Matthew Browne, 1880, pp. 77-85.—*North American Review*, by Eugene L. Didier, March 1880, pp. 302-306.—*Westminster Review*, April 1880, pp. 423-448 ; same article, *Littell's Living Age*, June 1880, pp. 707-720.—*Dublin Review*, by Helen Atteridge, April 1880, pp. 409-438.—*Month*, by the Rev. G. Macleod, May 1880, pp. 81-97. — *International Review*, by J. S. Morse, Jnn., vol. 8, p. 271.
——Life and Letters of. *Catholic World*, vol. 30, pp. 692-701.
——Little Boys and Great Men. *Little Folks*, by C. L. M. Nos. 64, 65.
- ——Little Dorrit. *Edinburgh Review*, July 1857, pp. 124-156.—*Leader*, June 1857, pp. 316, 617. — *Sun*, by Charles Kent, June 26, 1857.
——Lives of the Illustrious. *The Biographical Magazine*, by J. II. F., vol. 2, pp. 276-297.
—— Manuscripts. *Chambers's Journal*, Nov. 1877, pp. 710-712 ; same article, *Eclectic Magazine*, 1878, pp. 80-82 ; *Littell's Living Age*, 1878, pp. 252-254. — *Potter's American Monthly*, vol. 10, p. 156.
——Life and adventures of Martin Chuzzlewit. *Monthly Review*, Sept. 1844, pp. 137-146.—

Dickens, Charles.

National Review, July 1861, pp. 134-150.
——Master Humphrey's Clock. *Monthly Review*, May 1840, pp.35-43.—*Christian Examiner*, March 1842, pp. 1-19.
——Memories of Charles Dickens. *Atlantic Monthly*, by J. T. Fields, Aug. 1870, pp. 235-245 ; same article, *Piccadilly Annual*, 1870, pp. 66-72.
——Bygone Celebrities : II. Mr. Nightingale's Diary. *Gentleman's Magazine*, by R. H. Horne. May 1871, pp. 660-672.
——Modern Novelists. *Westminster Review*, Oct. 1864, pp. 414-441 ; same article, *Eclectic Magazine*, 1865, pp. 42-59.
——Modern Novels. Including the " Pickwick Papers, " "Nicholas Nickleby," and "Master Humphrey's Clock." *Christian Remembrancer*, Dec. 1842, pp. 581-596.
——Moral Services to Literature. *Spectator*, April 1869, pp. 474, 475 ; same article, *Eclectic Magazine*, July 1869, pp.103-106.
——Mystery of Edwin Drood. *Graphic*, April 1870, p. 438.— *Every Saturday*, 1870, vol. 9, pp. 291, 594.—*Spectator*, 1870, pp. 1176, 1177.—*Old and New*, (by George B. Woods), Nov. 1870, pp. 530-533. — *Southern Magazine*, 1873, vol. 14, p. 219. —*Belgravia* (by Thomas Foster), June 1878, pp. 453-473.
—— How " Edwin Drood " was Illustrated. [Illustrated.] *Century Magazine*, by Alice Meynell, Feb. 1884, pp. 522-528.
——A Quasi-Scientific Inquiry into "The Mystery of Edwin

Dickens, Charles.

Drood. Illustrated. *Knowledge,* by Thomas Foster, Sep. 12, Nov. 14, 1884.

——Suggestions for a Conclusion to "Edwin Drood." *Cornhill Magazine,* March 1884, pp. 308-317.

——Edwin Drood. Concluded by Charles Dickens, through a Medium. *Transatlantic,* vol. 2, 1873, pp. 173-183.

——In France. (Acting of Nicholas Nickleby in Paris.) *Fraser's Magazine,* March 1842, pp. 342-352.

—— Nomenclature. *Belgravia,* by W. F. Peacock, 1873, pp. 267-276, 393-402.

——Notes and Correspondence. *Englishwoman's Domestic Magazine,* vol. 11, 1871, pp. 91-95.

——Novel Reading: The works of. *Nineteenth Century,* by Anthony Trollope, 1879, pp. 24-43.

——Novels and Novelists. *North American Review,* by E. P. Whipple, October 1849, pp. 383-407; reprinted in "Literature and Life," etc., by E. P. Whipple.

——Old Curiosity Shop, Barnaby Rudge. *Christian Remembrancer,* vol. 4, 1842, p. 581. —*Pall Mall Gazette,* January 1, 1884, pp. 11, 12.

——The Old Lady of Fetter Lane (Old Curiosity Shop). (Illustrated.) *Pall Mall Gazette,* January 5, 1884, p.

——Oliver Twist. *Southern Literary Messenger,* May 1837, pp. 323-325.—*London and Westminster Review,* July 1837, pp. 194-215. — *Dublin University Magazine,* December 1838, pp.

Dickens, Charles.

699-723. — *Quarterly Review,* June 1839, pp. 83-102.—*Christian Examiner,* by J. S. D., Nov. 1839, pp. 161-174.— *Atlantic Monthly,* by Edwin P. Whipple, Oct. 1876, pp. 474-479.

——On Bells. *Belgravia,* by George Delamere Cowan, Jan. 1876, pp. 380-387.

——Our Letter. *St. Nicholas,* by M. F. Armstrong, 1877, pp. 438-441.

——Our Mutual Friend. *Eclectic Review,* Nov. 1865, pp. 455-476. —*Nation,* Dec. 1865, pp. 786, 787. — *Westminster Review,* April 1866, pp. 582-585.

——Our Mutual Friend in Manuscript. *Scribner's Monthly Magazine,* by Kate Field, August 1874, pp. 472-475.

——Pickwick Club. *Southern Literary Messenger,* 1836, pp. 787, 788; Sept. 1837, pp. 525-532.—*Littell's Museum of Foreign Literature,* vol. 32, 1837, p. 195.—*Monthly Review,* Feb. 1837, pp. 153-163.— *Eclectic Review,* April 1837, pp. 339-355.—*Chambers's Edinburgh Journal,* April 1837, pp. 109, 110.—*London and Westminster Review,* July 1837, pp. 194-215.—*Quarterly Review,* Oct. 1837, pp. 484-518.— *Belgravia,* by W. S. (W. Sawyer), July 1870, pp. 33-36. —*Atlantic Monthly,* by Edwin P. Whipple, Aug. 1876, pp. 219-224.

—— —— Mr. Pickwick and Nicholas Nickleby. [Illustrated.] *Scribner's Monthly,* by B. E. Martin, Sept. 1880, pp. 641-656.

—— ——From Faust to Mr. Pickwick. *Contemporary Re-*

Dickens, Charles.

view, by Matthew Browne, July 1880, pp. 162-176.

—— ——German Translation of the "Pickwick Papers." *Dublin Review,* Feb. 1840, pp. 160-188.

—— ——The Origin of the Pickwick Papers. *Society,* by R. H. Shepherd, Oct. 4, 1884, pp. 18-20.

—— ——The Portrait of Mr. Pickwick. *Belgravia,* by George Augustus Sala, Aug. 1870, pp. 165-171.

——Pictures from Italy. *Tait's Edinburgh Magazine,* vol. 13, 1846, pp. 461-466.—*Chambers's Edinburgh Journal,* 1846, pp. 389-391.—*Dublin Review,* Sept. 1846, pp. 184-201.—*Sun,* by Charles Kent, March 1846.

——Poetic Element in the Style of. *Every Saturday,* vol. 9, p. 811.

——The Pressmen of, and Thackeray. *Graphic,* by T. H. North, 1881, p. 116.

——Reception of. *United States Magazine and Democratic Review* (portrait), April 1842, pp. 315-320.

——Reminiscences of. *Englishwoman's Domestic Magazine,* by E. E. C., vol. 10, 1871, pp. 336-344.

——Remonstrance with. *Blackwood's Edinburgh Magazine,* April 1857, pp. 490-503 ; same article, *Littell's Living Age,* May 1857, pp. 480-492.

——Sale of the Effects of. *Every Saturday,* vol. 9, p. 557.— *Chambers's Journal,* 1870, pp. 522-505.

——Seasonable Words about.

Dickens, Charles.

The Overland Monthly, by N. S. Dodge, 1871, pp. 72-82.

——Secularistic Teaching. *Secular Chronicle,* by Harriet T. Law (portrait). Dec. 1877, pp. 289-291.

——Shadow on Life of. *Atlantic Monthly,* by Edwin P. Whipple, Aug. 1877, pp. 227-233.

——Sketches by Boz. *Monthly Review,* March 1836, pp. 350-357 ; 1837, pp. 153-163.— *Mirror,* April 1836, pp. 249-250.—*London and Westminster Review,* July 1837, pp. 194-215. —*Quarterly Review,* Oct. 1837, pp. 484-518.

—— ——The Boarding House (Sketches by Boz). *Chambers's Edinburgh Journal,* April 1836, pp. 83, 84.

—— ——Watkins Tottle and other Sketches (Sketches by Boz). *Southern Literary Messenger,* 1836, pp. 457-460.

——Son talent et ses œuvres. *Revue des Deux Mondes,* by H. Taine. Feb. 1856, pp. 618-647.

——Studien über Dickens und den Humor. *Westermann's Jahrbuch der Illustrirten Deutschen Monatshefte,* Von Julian Schmidt (portrait), April-July 1870.

——Studies of English Authors. No. V. Charles Dickens. In eleven chapters. *Literary World,* by Peter Bayne, March 21 to May 30, 1879.

——Study. *Graphic* Christmas Number, by C. C. 1870.

——A Tale of Two Cities. *Saturday Review,* Dec. 1859, pp. 741-743; same article, *Littell's Living Age,* Feb. 1860, pp. 366-369.—

Dickens, Charles.

Sun, by Charles Kent, Aug. 11, 1859.

——Tales. *Edinburgh Review,* Oct. 1838, pp. 75-97.

——The Tendency of Works of. *Argosy,* by A. D., 1885, pp. 282-292.

——The Tension in. *Every Saturday,* Dec. 1872, pp. 678-679.

——A Tramp with. Through London by Night with the Great Novelist. *Detroit Free Press,* April 7, 1883.

——Tulrumble, and Oliver Twist. *Southern Literary Messenger,* May 1837, pp. 323-325.

——The "Two Green Leaves" (portrait). *Graphic,* March 26, 1870, pp. 388-390.

——Unpublished Letters. *Times,* Oct. 27, 1883.

——Satire on. *Blackwood's Magazine,* by S. Warren, vol. 60, 1846, pp. 590-605; same article, *Eclectic Magazine,* vol. 10, 1847, p. 65.

——Use of the Bible. *Temple Bar,* September 1869, pp. 225-234; same article, *Appleton's Journal,* Oct. 16, 23, 1869, pp. 265-267, 294, 295; *Every Saturday,* vol. 8, p. 411.

——Verse. *Spectator,* 1877, pp. 1651-1653; same article, *Littell's Living Age,* 1878, pp. 237-241.

——Visit to Charles Dickens by Hans Christian Andersen.

Dickens, Charles.

Bentley's Miscellany, 1860, pp. 181-185; same article, *Littell's Living Age,* 1860, pp. 692-695, *Eclectic Magazine,* 1864, pp. 110-114.

—— —— Andersen's. *Temple Bar,* December 1870, pp. 27-46; same article, *Eclectic Magazine,* 1871, pp. 183-196, *Every Saturday,* vol. 9, p. 874, etc.; Appendix to *Pictures of Travels in Sweden,* etc.

—— ——Pilgrimage. [Visit to Gadshill.] *Lippincott's Magazine,* by Barton Hill. Sept. 1870, pp. 288-293.

——Voice of Christmas Past. (Illustrated.) *Harper's New Monthly Magazine,* by Mrs. Z. B. Buddington, January 1871, pp. 187-200.

——With the Newsvendors. — *Every Saturday,* vol. 9. p. 318.

——Works. *London University Magazine,* by J. S. (James Spedding), vol. 1, 1842, pp. 378-398.—*North British Review,* by J. Cleghorn, May 1845, pp. 65-87; same article, *Littell's Living Age,* June 1845, pp. 601-610.—*National Quarterly Review,* by H. Dennison, 1860, vol. 1, p. 91.—*British Quarterly Review,* Jan. 1862, pp. 135-159. —*Scottish Review,* Dec. 1883, pp 125-147.

VI.—CHRONOLOGICAL LIST OF WORKS.

Sketches by Boz .	. 1836-37	Martin Chuzzlewit.	.	1844
Sunday under Three		The Chimes .	.	1845
Heads . . .	1836	Cricket on the Hearth	.	1846
The Village Coquettes .	1836	Pictures from Italy	.	1846
The Strange Gentle-		Battle of Life .	.	1846
man	1837	Dombey and Son .	.	1848
Pickwick Papers .	. 1837	Haunted Man .	.	1848
Oliver Twist .	. 1838	David Copperfield .	.	1850
Sketches of Young		Mr. Nightingale's		
Gentlemen. . .	1838	Diary . . .		1851
Memoirs of Joseph		Child's History of		
Grimaldi . . .	1838	England . . .		1852-4
Nicholas Nickleby .	1839	Bleak House . .		1853 —
Sketches of Young		Hard Times .	.	1854 —
Couples . . .	1840	Little Dorrit . .	.	1857
Master Humphrey's		Hunted Down .	.	1859
Clock (The Old		Tale of Two Cities	.	1859
Curiosity Shop and		Great Expectations	.	1861 —
Barnaby Rudge) .	1840-1	Uncommercial Traveller.		1861
American Notes .	. 1842	Our Mutual Friend	.	1865
Christmas Carol .	. 1843	Mystery of Edwin Drood		1870

The Canterbury Poets.

EDITED BY WILLIAM SHARP.

WITH INTRODUCTORY NOTICES BY VARIOUS CONTRIBUTORS

In SHILLING Monthly Volumes, Square 8vo. Well printed on fine toned paper, with Red-line Border, and strongly bound in Cloth. Each Volume contains from 300 to 350 pages.

Cloth, Red Edges	- 1s.	Red Roan, Gilt Edges 2s. 6d.	
Cloth, Uncut Edges	- 1s.	Pad. Morocco, Gilt Edges - 5s.	

THE FOLLOWING VOLUMES ARE NOW READY.

London : WALTER SCOTT, 24 Warwick Lane, Paternoster Row.

Monthly Shilling Volumes.   Cloth, cut or uncut edges.

GREAT WRITERS.

EDITED BY PROFESSOR E. S. ROBERTSON.

THE FOLLOWING VOLUMES ARE NOW READY.

LIFE OF LONGFELLOW. By Professor Eric S. Robertson.
" A most readable little work, brightened by fancy, and enriched by poetic
feeling."—*Liverpool Mercury.*

LIFE OF COLERIDGE. By Hall Caine.
" Brief and vigorous, written throughout with spirit and great literary
skill, often rising into eloquence."—*Scotsman.*

LIFE OF DICKENS. By Frank T. Marzials.
" We should, until we came across this volume, have been at a loss to
recommend any popular life of England's most popular novelist as being
really satisfactory."—*Athenæum.*

LIFE OF DANTE GABRIEL ROSSETTI. By Joseph Knight.
" Mr. Knight's picture of the great poet and painter is the fullest and best
yet presented to the public."—*The Graphic.*

LIFE OF SAMUEL JOHNSON. By Colonel F. Grant.
" Colonel Grant has performed his task with diligence, sound judgment,
good taste, and accuracy."—*Illustrated London News.*

LIFE OF DARWIN, By G. T. Bettany.
"Mr. G. T. Bettany's *Life of Darwin* is a sound and conscientious work."
—*Saturday Review.*

LIFE OF CHARLOTTE BRONTE. By Augustine Birrell.
" Those who know much of Charlotte Brontë will learn more, and those
who know nothing about her will find all that is best worth learning in Mr.
Birrell's pleasant book."—*St. James' Gazette.*

LIFE OF THOMAS CARLYLE. By Richard Garnett, LL.D.
" This is an admirable book. Nothing could be more felicitous and fairer
than the way in which he takes us through Carlyle's life and works."—*Pall
Mall Gazette.*

LIFE OF ADAM SMITH. By R. B. Haldane, M.P.
" Written throughout with a perspicuity seldom exemplified when dealing
with economic science."—*Scotsman.*

LIFE OF KEATS. By W. M. Rossetti.
" Valuable for the ample information which it contains and the
sympathetic and authoritative criticism which it furnishes."—*Cambridge
Independent.*

LIFE OF SHELLEY. By William Sharp.
" Another fit memorial of a beautiful soul. . . . it is a worthy addition,
to be cherished for its own sake to our already rich collection of Shelley
Literature."—*The Academy.*

LIFE OF SMOLLETT. By David Hannay.
" An exceptionally manly and capable record."—*Saturday Review.*

LIFE OF GOLDSMITH. By Austin Dobson.
LIFE OF SCOTT. By Professor Yonge.
LIFE OF BURNS. By Professor Blackie.
LIFE OF VICTOR HUGO. By Frank T. Marzials.
LIFE OF EMERSON. By Richard Garnett, LL.D.
LIFE OF GOETHE. By James Sime.
LIFE OF CONGREVE. By Edmund Gosse.
LIFE OF BUNYAN. By Canon Venables.
LIFE OF CRABBE. By T. E. Kebbel, M.A.   [*Ready September 25th.*

Complete Bibliography to each volume, by J. P. ANDERSON, British Museum.

LIBRARY EDITION OF "GREAT WRITERS."—Printed on
large paper of extra quality, in handsome binding, Demy 8vo, price 2s. 6d.

London : WALTER SCOTT, 24 Warwick Lane, Paternoster Row.

RE-ISSUE IN MONTHLY VOLUMES, PRICE ONE SHILLING EACH,

STRONGLY BOUND IN CLOTH,

Uniform in size and style with the Camelot Series,

WILSON'S
TALES OF THE BORDERS

AND OF SCOTLAND:

HISTORICAL, TRADITIONARY, AND IMAGINATIVE.

REVISED BY ALEXANDER LEIGHTON.

No collection of tales published in a serial form ever enjoyed so great a popularity as " THE TALES OF THE BORDERS ; " and the secret of their success lies in the fact that they are stories in the truest sense of the word, illustrating in a graphic and natural style the manners and customs, trials and sorrows, sins and backslidings, of the men and women of whom they treat. The heroes and heroines of these admirable stories belong to every rank of life, from the king and noble to the humble peasant.

"THE TALES OF THE BORDERS" have always been immensely popular with the young, and whether we view them in their moral aspect, or as vehicles for instruction and amusement, the collected series forms a repertory of healthy and interesting literature unrivalled in the language.

The *Scotsman* says :—"Those who have read the tales in the unwieldy tomes in which they are to be found in the libraries will welcome the publication of this neat, handy, and well-printed edition."

The *Dundee Advertiser* says :—"Considering how attractive are these tales, whether regarded as illustrating Scottish life, or as entertaining items of romance, there can be no doubt of their continued popularity. We last read them in volumes the size of a family Bible, and we are glad to have an opportunity to renew our acquaintance with them in a form so much more handy and elegant."

EACH VOLUME WILL BE COMPLETE IN ITSELF.

London : WALTER SCOTT, 24 Warwick Lane, Paternoster Row.

Windsor Series of Poetical Anthologies.

Printed on Antique Paper. Crown 8vo. Bound in Blue Cloth,
each with suitable Emblematic Design on Cover, Price 3s. 6d.
Also in various Calf and Morocco Bindings.

Women's Voices. An Anthology of the
most Characteristic Poems by English, Scotch, and Irish Women.
Edited by Mrs. William Sharp.

Sonnets of this Century. With an
Exhaustive and Critical Essay on the Sonnet. Edited by
William Sharp.

The Children of the Poets. An Anthology
from English and American Writers of Three Centuries. Edited
by Professor Eric S. Robertson.

Sacred Song. A Volume of Religious
Verse. Selected and arranged, with Notes, by Samuel
Waddington.

A Century of Australian Song. Selected
and Edited by Douglas B. W. Sladen, B.A., Oxon.

Jacobite Songs and Ballads. Selected
and Edited, with Notes, by G. S. Macquoid.

Irish Minstrelsy. Edited, with Notes and
Introduction, by H. Halliday Sparling.

The Sonnets of Europe. A Volume of
Translations. Selected and arranged, with Notes, by Samuel
Waddington.

Early English and Scottish Poetry.
Selected and Edited, with Introduction and Notes, by H.
Macaulay Fitzgibbon.

Ballads of the North Countrie. Edited,
with Introduction, by Graham R. Tomson.

Songs and Poems of the Sea. An
Anthology of Poems Descriptive of the Sea. Edited by Mrs.
William Sharp.

Songs and Poems of Fairyland. An
Anthology of English Fairy Poetry, selected and arranged, with
an Introduction, by Arthur Edward Waite.

London: WALTER SCOTT, 24 Warwick Lane, Paternoster Row

THE OXFORD LIBRARY.

Strongly Bound in Elegant Cloth Binding, Price 2s. each.

This Series of Popular Books comprises many original Novels by new Authors, as well as the most choice works of Dickens, Lytton, Smollett Scott, Ferrier, etc.

The following are now ready, and will be followed by others shortly:—

BARNABY RUDGE.	ETHEL LINTON.
OLD CURIOSITY SHOP.	A MOUNTAIN DAISY.
PICKWICK PAPERS.	HAZEL; or, Perilpoint Lighthouse.
NICHOLAS NICKLEBY.	VICAR OF WAKEFIELD.
OLIVER TWIST.	PRINCE of the HOUSE of DAVID.
MARTIN CHUZZLEWIT.	WIDE, WIDE WORLD.
SKETCHES BY BOZ.	VILLAGE TALES.
RODERICK RANDOM.	BEN-HUR.
PEREGRINE PICKLE.	UNCLE TOM'S CABIN.
IVANHOE.	ROBINSON CRUSOE.
KENILWORTH.	CHARLES O'MALLEY.
JACOB FAITHFUL.	MIDSHIPMAN EASY.
PETER SIMPLE.	BRIDE OF LAMMERMOOR.
PAUL CLIFFORD.	HEART OF MIDLOTHIAN.
EUGENE ARAM.	LAST OF THE BARONS.
ERNEST MALTRAVERS.	OLD MORTALITY.
ALICE ; or, the Mysteries.	TOM CRINGLE'S LOG.
RIENZI.	CRUISE OF THE MIDGE.
PELHAM.	COLLEEN BAWN.
LAST DAYS OF POMPEII.	VALENTINE VOX.
THE SCOTTISH CHIEFS.	NIGHT AND MORNING.
WILSON'S TALES.	FOXE'S BOOK OF MARTYRS.
THE INHERITANCE.	BUNYAN'S PILGRIM'S PROGRESS.

London : WALTER SCOTT, 24 Warwick Lane, Paternoster Row.

CROWN 8vo, 440 *PAGES, PRICE ONE SHILLING.*

THE WORLD

OF CANT.

"*Daily Telegraph.*"—"Decidedly a book with a purpose."

"*Scotsman.*"—"A vigorous, clever, and almost ferocious exposure, in the form of a story, of the numerous shams and injustices."

"*Newcastle Weekly Chronicle.*"—"Trenchant in sarcasm, warm in commendation of high purpose. . . . A somewhat *remarkable book.*"

"*London Figaro.*"—"It cannot be said that the author is partial; clergymen and Nonconformist divines, Liberals and Conservatives, lawyers and tradesmen, all come under his lash. . . . The sketches are worth reading. Some of the characters are portrayed with considerable skill."

"May the Lord deliver us from all Cant: may the Lord, whatever else He do or forbear, teach us to look facts honestly in the face, and to beware (with a kind of shudder) of smearing them over with our despicable and damnable palaver into irrecognisability, and so falsifying the Lord's own Gospels to His unhappy blockheads of Children, all staggering down to Gehenna and the everlasting Swine's-trough, for want of Gospels.

"O Heaven! it is the most accursed sin of man: and done everywhere at present, on the streets and high places at noonday! Verily, seriously I say and pray as my chief orison, May the Lord deliver us from it."—*Letter from Carlyle to Emerson.*

London : WALTER SCOTT, 24 Warwick Lane, Paternoster Row.

www.ingramcontent.com/pod-product-compliance
Lightning Source LLC
Chambersburg PA
CBHW020625030726
47497CB00007B/2425